Our Lady of the Outfield

by

David Craig

author: The Cheese Stands Alone

Our Lady of the Outfield
A Novel
By David Craig

ISBN #1891280058

Library of Congress Catalog Card Number: 99-066954

Manufactured in the United States of America.

CMJ Marian Publisher, INC.
P.O. Box 661
Oak Lawn, Illinois 60454
www.cmjbooks.com

Acknowledgments

I'd like to thank Thomas Kelly whose SUMMER OF '54 provided the quasi-historical baseline of wons and losses which made this music possible, the Hahns for their book ROME SWEET ROME which gave me some helpful technical language and a good example of a struggling Protestant wife. I'd also like to thank Mark Miravalle and his research assistant for a run-down of contemporary Marian apparitions, and John Phillips, a great neighbor and ex-sportswriter, for his tips around the batting cage.

And finally, especially, I'd like to thank Linda for all her support.

Also, please note that the author used great restraint in not subtitling this "THE GREATEST BASEBALL STORY EVERY TOLD."

Narrators:
JOSEPH, angel second class
MONEY, sportswriter

I.

JOSEPH:

His parents, like almost every other flickering soul in their sleepy little northern California town, were not Catholic. They were what might be called dyed-in-the-spirit Unitarians, strolling through the Sundays of their American lives. They were so much a part of the times in which they lived; the Wells happily did the expected for the most part. Mom baked pies and kept a sharp lookout for her little boy, her hands wringing in the lap of her red and white checkered apron as she peered out the window.

Pa Wells was a mechanic, owned a little shop on Main Street, still smoked marijuana after all these years. His hair, long and faded gold, pony-tailed in the back, his wispy beard, were all testament to the times he longed for, an imaginary past filled with gentle buzzes: the half-sleepy bees on idyllic Saturday mornings.

On Fridays the eagle, as they say, spoke its piece. It was down to the Dew Drop Inn for Buds, beer and his pals, some spirited conversation, the Mrs. sometimes joining him for a lively game of bowling, fifty cents for two plays. They tagged-teamed the neighborhood, both slightly lit and laughing as they'd walk home under a calm summer moon, talking about the games, their lives, their baby.

If grace was anywhere in evidence back then to them, it was within the coverlet of those warm summer nights where nothing much happened outside of the creaking hooks of front porch swings, some intimate gossip, and the loud peal of laughter which often followed in the twilight. It could be heard in the occasional distant barking of a dog, seen in the lightning bugs, a few neighborhood kids with glasses to catch them in, Keith included. And later, well into the dark, games of hide 'n seek around the eucalyptus in the front yard, only one resident during those earlier years actually embracing a tree.

There were a few old junkers in various modes of disrepair in the high weeds next to their little square house. They provided atmosphere. Of course the clotheslined Boxer, Zeke, the penned goat whose name changed with the seasons, the amount of milk she gave didn't hurt either.

Keith found the recreation he needed beyond his family's property line. In a stand of trees out back he'd pump .22 caliber pellets into coke cans or at birds when he was feeling contrary. His mother, more supportive than most, assisted him by saving up cans, buying gun oil. From the very beginning she had decided to keep the home-light burning, whatever the personal expense. She had her hands on every knob in the steam shovel cabin, even joined the PTA when Keith was in junior high because she felt it was her duty to do so.

And as for speaking her mind, well, that had never been a problem for Julia Wells. With her loosely-tied hair, her earth woman clothes, she mounted a one woman lobby for computers in the schools long before they were in vogue, unsuccessfully picketed for a baseball team batting cage. She was the first woman on the block to own an aerobics video.

Her marriage and family were in her eyes the most accurate measures of who she was. She held onto them like death because of her own lonely early years. Her home had been broken by her thirty-five year old mother who, having run away herself when she was only fourteen, caught the slightest whiff of the failing sixties, and, sorrow or sorrows, found herself facing middle age with no meaningful counter-cultural experiences to show for it. As a result she soaked up its every waning minute nuance, as if her own family life provided her with nothing she needed. Eventually she left home, still in some way fourteen, in a last ditch sorrowful effort to find her own "space" as she put it, in the great and beneficent outdoors.

"Good luck and fat chance," her grown daughter said reflectively, all these years later, deeply inhaling her Virgina Slim. "Hell, she had enough space between her ears to keep her busy for centuries."

There had been the occasional letter, none with return addresses. The last Julia and her father had heard, her mother was living in a teepee, smoking the good earth, urging them both to become more craft-oriented.

Pulling a shred of tobacco from her mouth at that point, Julia thought about her lonesome teenage years, something she would not allow to happen here. Kids needed a mom, whatever the daily talk-show ditzes said.

But to her credit, thoughtful homemaker that she was, she was careful not to over-react either. She'd seen that performance before, too, kept some of her mother's "underground" books, just to peruse occasionally, weigh against what she had gathered from other sources.

She was, for the most part, a sincere woman, and if she hadn't found the meaning of life for herself yet, she felt she could intuitively decide in what direction it lay. Eyes on the future, she kept her boy in line, in love, as happy and "well-adjusted" as she could.

And Gerry, the old man, he was easy, enjoyed "going with the flow." Less friction that way. Besides, she gave him room enough for the most part, and he liked feeling protected, though he never would have admitted to that. He liked it, the whole domestic scene: her warm arm around his sometimes when he came through the door, food on the table, candles once in awhile, a candy dish. It was a good deal. He never had that kind of thing when he was growing up. His own Mom had to work from the time he was very young as she tried to make up for the Dad he'd never known, who'd been lost in Korea. He loved his wife, liked the situation, always made sure he came to meals with his hands clean.

Keith came to baseball later than most, introduced by his Evangelical girlfriend who played in a fast-pitch softball church league. He took to it like a duck, wiggling his tail in new water, and within a year helped his father to construct a chicken wire batting cage in their backyard, some canvas rolled and tied across the top so he could practice even during the wet Northern California winter months.

The pitching machine itself was an old one; his Dad had gotten it used and oiled it, made new parts in his little garage. He gave it to his son for his 16th birthday.

And though he had no special interest in the game, Keith's father often went out to watch his son after work. He even bought a few books: Ted Williams on hitting, would put his opened beer under his arm and page through them, just to offer what he hoped would be helpful hints as his son worked to find his rhythm. Julia would bring out dinner with a flashlight when things got to her way of thinking too dark. (Eventually they set up a string of Japanese lanterns around the cage. Mom would flick them on and off when she could barely see him.) She worried though and asked him about the things she thought he might be missing: dances, drag races, rock 'n roll music.

But her son was elsewhere. He was joyfully obsessed, wanted to start at shortstop during his senior year. And in an effort to prepare himself for that, he put a chinning bar in his bedroom doorway to improve his arm strength, did isometrics every night. He even braved his fellow students' disdain by enrolling in a ballet class at a local community college that winter just to strengthen his legs, to improve his leaping ability around the bag.

And his efforts were rewarded. Halfway through his senior year, pro and college scouts, those time-honored migratory birds of opportunity, began to find this year's Capistranos. They sought him after school, in the halls, in front of his locker. They smiled at him from behind backstops, talked to him late in parking lots, he in his soiled socks, hungry for dinner. They would call early in the morning, arrange to meet the family.

Julia beamed inside. She had long felt that there was something special about her son, and all the current attention only seemed to confirm this. But she did what she could to hide that fact. She wanted in the worst way to help him realize his dreams, but she knew too that he was not a son to these people. He was a commodity, a possibility. And so she watched every interloper with the intensity of a mother eagle.

Demanding civility, she always insisted that the visitor in question contribute something when he came: Napa wines, crepes, an exotic fruit. And she wouldn't let anyone talk baseball until they engaged in some lengthy general conversation first. The weather, politics, the man's family. Those were her ground rules and everyone abided by them.

He was as graceful a shortstop as any of them had seen in years, and he hit as if he'd been born to the task. Watching him swing, one couldn't help but feel how much of him was invested in the process. He was like some kind of powerful, uncomfortable machine, graceful here too, but making noises, falling over himself, off balance, emitting sweat, smiles, release valve steam. There was a grace-filled joy in living physically there, and everyone picked up on it.

A few of the balls he hit that spring were actually lost, became the subject of myth as some of the neighboring high school parks had no fences. Games were delayed as outfielders leafed their ways through the woods, throwing out the occasional golf ball, empty coke can to reclining teammates. One fellow never came back. The scouts shook their heads: California.

Smack. Smack. Ping. One after another, with his aluminum bat in hands, he lined each pitch back toward its point of origin. Baseballs clanged off the old machine, shook it, seemed to give it life as it sputtered and spit like something out of an old cartoon. Balls rebounded off of the wooden support posts which his father and he had cemented into the lawn. Sometimes, if he pulled the ball too much, he'd have to hop out of the way, or attempt to do as much as one would ricochet off the nearest side post and come right back at him.

His mom got him a batting helmet, just in case. She stood watching from outside the chicken-wire corridor on one particular day, placed the egg salad sandwiches inside at the first opportunity. As she assisted him in the gathering up of the balls into one of the buckets, she again tried to understand her son.

"I still don't see what you see in this stuff anyway. I don't understand," she said, frowning. "I mean, I can appreciate the physical part of it, but it all seems so pointless."

"Get hip, mom," he said, using just the kind of language his grandmother might have employed. (It was a joke he and his Mom both shared, enjoyed.) "It's a rush. Maxing out in the present. Om. Grandma would'a dug it. You can feel your success in your hands, each time you rip one. How often do you get a chance to do that in life? . . . Look, see," he said, showing her the marks on one of the baseballs. "Success written all over it."

"You're starting to scare me." They both laughed. "But what about your future? You can't really expect to do this for a living." She could tell, however, that this route of inquiry was leading nowhere and dropped it. "Is Katie coming over tonight? She seems like a nice girl . . . if you don't. . ."

"Count that Bible stuff. I know, Mom. But I don't mind checking it out, either. It's not like we've got any profound thing happening around here, is it?"

"Oh I don't know. Look at those trees in the breeze."

"What's that supposed to mean?"

She smiled. "Heck if I know." They both laughed. "This ought to last you till dinner. Then homework. . . I forgot. Did you say you were going to college or not?" She scratched her head. More laughter.

"We'll see, ma," he said as he began banging them out again.

Katie had a pleasing face, a cute nose. When he first saw her, she was admonishing co-workers on the gym bleachers about quality, three magic markers in her right hand, a huge roll of white paper at her feet. She sounded preppy to him, making suggestions, laughing expansively, her other hand occasionally, dramatically inverted on her hip. She talked about spacing, graphics, making the occasional humorous interjection about how sorely the squad was over-matched in the upcoming game.

He thought she looked like Maid Marian: the straight brown-blond hair, loosely tied back, the blue eyes, freckles, tanned complexion, high cheekbones. When she caught him looking at her, she responded unself-consciously, smiled.

They looked at each other for a long time, until both flushed. (They could never subsequently agree on who broke the gaze first.) But when she returned to work, she seemed now too conscious of her movements. He was charmed.

She was "a real Christian," as he put it to his mother, the sword to both their minds having two definite edges. But he found he did like her spirit, and he felt more peaceful in some way when he was around her. She was like him, always pushing, though not at him. He liked that. And if he didn't completely understand what was behind that for her, he did like the results. In her beach wagon she'd drive the two of them for miles to find the best winter waves; they'd don wet suits, break out the boards, the Hibachi. She introduced him to Tai food, sushi; they'd tour natural history museums, go ballooning, hang-gliding, snorkeling. After winter semester, they even tried their hands, at his insistence, at book burning, just to get a feel for repressive measures.

She didn't seem the Puritan to his mind, though; she knew how to relax. After fast pitching underhanded to him in the late spring, he, hitting grounders to her, they'd "get horizontal" along side their Dr. Peppers. They'd enjoy the feel of breezes as each would brush over their separate perspiring forms, caress the beads of sweat that ran down their faces and their necks, the chill that moisture brought with it. The grasses waved and the clouds asked to be configured, the days drifting by.

They'd try to describe each sensation, and when one of them came up with an especially apt metaphor—the bead of sweat like the legs of a fly as it moved down her neck—there'd be groans, laughter.

On weekends they would usually go to her church for socials. He'd decided he would try to see what there was to it for her sake. And though he was no believer, he found that he could live with most of what they taught. The golden rule. Who couldn't agree with that? Granted, with his enemies it was asking a lot, more than he could probably deliver, but it was a nice, workable way of dealing with people he cared about.

And if their religion didn't answer all his questions, it did provide, as they put it, good fellowship. It was a bit on the square side, sure—Keith suggested to her one night that with the preacher's cubed head, he probably had to walk around the block to turn over in bed. But Katie was at home here and not pushy about his response to it.

Sex, thank the merciful Lord, was out of the question for her. She wouldn't hear of it. So he'd try to keep his mind on other things. And the church, having similar notions, kept the young people busy. Katie and Keith would go out with a lot of her church friends on especially designed Saturday recreations. Corny stuff mostly to his mind: haunted houses, camp fire sing-alongs, Bible hiking trips. But her off beat humor made it all interesting for him. The services as well. She'd comment on the preacher's mannerisms, or come up behind people he was speaking to, look bored just to make his strained conversation difficult.

And if he didn't know quite what to make of people waving their hands in the air, speaking in ancient languages, singing hymns, he didn't hold it against them either. It was no weirder than Grandma. And these guys let him know they were there for him. It was not anything he felt he needed at first, but he did appreciate their saying as much. So he'd close his eyes during the difficult parts, try to get into whatever spirit it was, sway.

Taken on the whole it wasn't such an unpleasant way to spend his weekends. The people were friendly and out-going. They'd go miles out of their ways to help you, get you great summer or weekend jobs. He liked all the people he met there, the whole scene, really, and his social nature quickly made him a valued and looked-for participant in church events.

"Hi, Mrs. Wells. We're back."

"So I see," Keith's mother replied. "Did anybody fall over this time? . . . I hope no one gets hurt there."

"No," Katie smiled. "It's called 'falling out,' getting 'slain in the Spirit,' but it wasn't that kind of service tonight. It was much more laid-back. Why don't you come with us next week? I'm sure you'd like it. It's non-denominational."

"No, not for me. At least not yet. I have my cookies, you know." Everyone smiled. "Here, have one as soon as they cool down."

"You should a seen this one, Mom," Keith said, stuffing two warm ones into his mouth. "It was one of those human things, everybody washing everybody else's feet. It made me cry." Katie punched him. "No, you should've seen this guy next to me; he had some pretty serious toe jam. . . . Here, I saved some." He began rummaging through his pockets.

Both women expressed revulsion, and so satisfied him. "You do have to admit it, though. That guy next to me had REALLY smelly feet. I mean, God, if you're going to come to a feet washing, you really ought to clean your feet, don't you think?"

"Maybe God was trying to tell you something," Katie said, though it quickly came to her that she had no idea what that might mean. Mother and son looked doubtful. She recovered. "Anyway they're all nice people, and the Lord IS being glorified."

"Okay. But I don't want any of this cult business," Julie warned.

"Oh, Mrs. Wells! It's not like that at all. . ."

But her defense was interrupted by Keith, who rather noisily had his head in the fridge. All both could hear were grunts and the clanking of jars and bottles. By the time he re-emerged, both hands and mouth were loaded: bagged lunch meat, cheeses, mustards, hot peppers and horse radish, bread, and milk. "Just a snack," he self-consciously mumbled through a plastic bag, looking humorously shocked at their slack-jawed, amazed faces.

"Mrs. Wells, how DO you put up with this guy?" Katie asked, giving him a hip as he passed by.

"I don't know, really," she said. "Keith, please, before you touch any of that—WASH YOUR HANDS!"

And before you could say Larry Doby, there they were again, out back, Katie reminding him about his hitch as each ball, jerked forward by the pitching arm, was sent back with grunts and sweat, accompanying what was for them both sweet music.

Keith went in the first third of the opening round, the second of Cleveland's picks that year and used the substantial bonus to buy his dad a complete tool chest, his very surprised mother a diamond-studded gold cross and chain. (He couldn't resist.) He celebrated for a week with Katie and some of his friends. Would have done more for everyone, spent the whole bundle had his parents not intervened. There was his future to think about.

He was two weeks out of high school when he took his first plane ride courtesy of the Cleveland Indians to Burlington, S. C., home of the Burlington Indians of the Appalachian Rookie League. He was full of youthful enthusiasm and excitement as he claimed his window seat, as he tried to feel the exact moment when the wheels lifted from the runway.

Once airborne, he watched the patchwork farms move by underneath him, the little lakes gleam in the sun, the tiny cars and trailers through two plates of plastic glass. After the serving cart had made its rounds, he decided to try the earphones in the sealed pouch in front of him.

He tore open the plastic bag and ripped through the channels, all thirteen of them, looking for some Patsy Cline or early Elvis.

Not knowing any better, he put the earphones on as one would a stereo set, the two cords becoming one above his head. He didn't know quite what to do with what was left, so he let the remaining plastic cord slope down to one side. And there he stayed, cruising through the channels, bobbing in his seat, making the occasional half-sung noise, a youthful connoisseur on life's pilgrimage, until a tactful stewardess, smiling broadly, motioned for him to pull the whole thing beneath his chin.

He smiled, lifted a speaker from his left ear: "I knew that."

A team official, a Mink Sunnydale, greeted him with a sign at the airport. He lavished praise on the young man as they drove around town: he told him how lucky they were to get him with that pick. The front office boys were sweating it there for awhile, big time, as the Cards and Dodgers had their eyes on him as well.

He kept talking, punctuated the praise, handing him his card, lists of housing options, bus schedules, several cards for reputable car dealers. Some renters in town offered six month leases just for players, Travel Lodge the best bet there. Keith, they really liked his swing, could stay with him for a few days before he got settled in, or Mink could help him get set up somewhere today. The Indians, as they had informed Keith by letter, would supply the spikes. But did he have any special needs: a particular brand of batting glove, types of wristbands? Did he need any jewelry?

Since Keith was a number one pick, Mink said he might be able to get him some of those things gratis in exchange for some radio time. Welcome to the professional ranks. Local sporting goods and jewelry stores were always up for that sort of thing.

The older man told him about what he might expect. The manager was a good guy, but could come across a little gruff on occasion. Don't let that bother you. Practices started at 10:00, sometimes two-a-day at the beginning. Just be yourself; try to have a little fun. Work hard.

Keith signed a rental agreement for an unfurnished two-bedroom, with Mink, a true and too conscious patron of opportunity, still talking, this time to the owner, at his side. "Take care of this kid for us, now. He's a real blue-chipper; make sure he gets to practice." It all made Keith feel good, valued, as he was sure it was meant to. And sifting through the material he had been given, he pocketed the bus schedules and dealership cards, shook both their hands and headed across the parking lot with his new luggage. He'd find the laundry room and incinerator himself.

Once inside the empty apartment, he pulled the shower curtain back, opened a few windows, and stuck his head and arms out one to catch the rest of the complex. Trees moved beyond the lot in the southern breeze. When he came back through, he placed the bags he had dropped right in the middle of the empty living room and decided as he sorted through the bus schedules that it was time to meet the natives.

He walked all over the town that afternoon, stopped in every quaint shop he found. Talking to anyone who approached him, he gathered some of the town's history, its tastes, and its people. He eventually settled on a bank, bought a radio, rode every bus available, ending his first day by eating where he found the most local color.

It was a diner called Betty's. Old farmers in John Deere caps came in and out. As he waited for service, he listened to the conversations, the accents, thick as what? A clot of pollen maybe or the heavy sag of August leaves. As thick as the collar of heat that pressed down on him as he walked to wavering asphalt in this Southern town. That much was sure.

Maybe that's what made them talk that way. He wondered what Katie would have come up with as he ordered a cherry pie. The large waitress in her hospital whites was nice, pouring coffee refills for everybody in sight, all the while carrying on several conversations simultaneously. She had to duck each time she went through one section to avoid a heating duct. All done with dexterity. It was a new world all right, a world where he would have to find his place.

During the first practice he actively sought his new teammates, tried to meet as many as possible. Putting his hat on backwards, he tagged his introductions with, "Perhaps you've heard of me," just to loosen things up, set the tone. It worked here as it always had, and he became an immediate favorite, sought for a quip or used as an example as he exuded friendship, humor, and a cooperative spirit.

He enjoyed the practices for the most part, the cleanly manicured field, the advertisements on the outfield fences — one for a place called Happy Church—birds singing in the trees beyond the grandstands. But they could go on, those practices. In some ways they were like every practice he had ever gone to, a never-ending battle with fundamentals, although there were more of them here. The coaching staff offered instruction in bunting and sliding, the players hit before instructors off a tee, they worked on hit-and-runs, run-and-hits, they worked on cut-off alignments, on fielding technique, on backing each other up, on every possible double play, on pick-offs, on sign sequences. At the end of the first session, the manager introduced a front-office guy to them who talked deportment and professionalism, all to thirty very young people, each in leisurely decline, on the outfield grass.

Keith was switched to second base by the third practice, so he welcomed the extra fundamental time, at least for awhile. It was part of the necessary work they all knew they had to put in. And the coaches, knowing as well the difficulty in sustaining interest on the part of the players, did what they could to lighten the atmosphere. They encouraged humor of any sort, usually tried to end things on an up note: ground ball, home-run derbies, insisting all the while, too loudly, that wagering would not be a good habit to get into here.

There were lots of hoots during those events, as each dying horse was ridden unmercifully to its grave. It was baseball, after all, a bunch of forever-boys taking mutual delight in the privilege that comes with participation. But there was more than that happening here. Each player was finding his way into the pecking order, each becoming, to use the cliché, part of a team.

As the weeks passed, Keith found himself more and more in the company of certain worldly rounders: a Bill Cassano and one Ron Punic, a catcher and outfielder respectively. They both were older than he, but that didn't seem to matter to any of them. Like most people, Bill and Ron valued, sadly, the diversion that a pleasant, bright, upbeat atmosphere can bring, and Keith was a good, if young, architect of that. Of course, Keith WAS a first rounder as well, but they were for the most part straight forward guys. They liked him. He had the prototypical athlete's sense of humor: heavy on the obvious irony. He could keep things on an acceptably superficial level, only bringing up anything substantial into a conversation if the situation absolutely demanded it, but even then, only around the edges, and only in the form of conventional wisdom. He, like too many people, didn't spend much time on the bigger life-and-spiritual-death issues; rather, he valued a crisp pace, a sense of fine distraction, especially in the company of other men.

Neither Ron nor Bill had taken an apartment immediately, both wanting to look around, get as they put it, the lay of the land first. Bill stayed in a middling motel and Ron, having cashed in his plane ticket, slept in the back of a beat Buick which he had driven all the way out from San Diego. Keith told them about his place; he was looking for some tidy roommates.

They moved in that afternoon with all the assurance of men several years older. And the three of them enjoyed the whole process: getting the hang of tying hastily-gathered furniture to the roof of a Riviera, of mattress bends and engineering decisions as they angled new and used furniture around corners, up stairs. They rummaged most of the day through large item trash, went to garage sales early the next morning. What they couldn't find there they bought at Sears or found in the TRI-COUNTY MERCHANDISER: two worn recliners, an American Eagle lamp, a dining room table and some chairs, two spittoons, a wooden Indian, blankets and beds, sheets and pillowcases.

A refrigerator and stove were already provided, so they figured they were set for six months, except, for perhaps, as Bill suggested, some needed ambiance. Maybe they should put up a few life-affirming posters, a lava lamp —the babes liked that kind of stuff.

Ron looked at him like he was from Mars, suggested Spanish Colonial. Or maybe Bill could get a life. The sixties were dead, deserved to be. Open the windows, he told him. Donna Summers might be out there.

When Keith suggested curtains, there was silence. What did they need them for Ron asked? Those were for women, though his exact expression was more crudely put. Besides, which of them was going to go into the domestics department and ask for them? Before you'd know it, one of them might actually be cooking.

But Keith, who was too young for much guile, would not easily be put off. What about towels, soap? Ron told him that was what locker rooms were for. Where had he been living all his life? Bill, the other half of the act, just shook his head, suggested that perhaps Ron needed to do some sensitivity training.

They were both anxious to help Keith find a car, sold him on an old Mustang with a rag top. Bill suggested, in his worldly way, that they could score like Bird in it. And Ron, never one to miss an adolescent opening, told Bill that he couldn't score if he went to umpire school.

The two of them made bets, continued harassing each other all the way home. Each of them had gone in the lower rounds. Ron, 22, a professional bartender, had been playing at a junior college that spring. He was young and, full of the attendant enthusiasm, figured that, what the hey, even if he didn't make it, minor league life could be something to tell his kids about. You couldn't win the lotto if you didn't play.

Bill was a stoutish 21 year old Italian with a big, ready smile, had graduated from Iowa State in May where he'd earned All-American honors. He told them how valuable catchers were. Besides, he wanted to make connections here: he'd majored in Sports Management, gave them each his card. Ron laughed, fished in his pocket for a ten spot. "Go get a us a twelve pack. Can ya manage that?"

After some weeks, Keith decided that Bill was as mad as Ron was, but at least he had a college man's reserve. The younger man enjoyed what they brought to his life: an apparently comfortable worldliness that seemed to offer freedom, the urgent sap of youth. He ran cracked and crazed along side them as they all stumbled, almost confidently, through their respective youths.

The two of them would occasionally rouse Keith late at night, get impromptu games of football together in the parking lot at two a.m., bang on friends' doors, men and women, to get them to play as well. They knew most of the girls in the complex, having met them while sunning at the pool after practices.

Keith would watch with amazement as Ron and Bill would surround any new woman they saw there. Those meat-market "games" were decided more quickly than most at-bats, and that made him shudder a little bit: how quickly each person sized up the other. You could almost hear the calculations; how good did the person look in his or her suit; what did he or she do for a living; how should I play this? All within the space of two minutes. "Sift and drift" was Bill's expression. And apparently, as far as Keith could see, it worked for the catcher. Before the season was over he'd met and stuck to a nice looking, wavy-permed stewardess.

The three of them would go to college bars in Chapel Hill, at Duke, offer summer coeds free tickets. There'd be impromptu swims, beer bottles on reservoir cliffs, road trips in packed cars; there'd be long late night sodden conversations, pairs occasionally splintering off, each going in their own direction, each looking for what they thought they would surely find.

Ron probably had the most questions because he took the most chances. He'd sneak into half-empty girls' dorms, run around asking for someone named Judy—that was all he'd gotten, no last name. He'd pull on a long face as if he were a pathetic character, as if she'd just met and dropped him, and he was really hurt.

It was his own unique approach: true need disguised as need. Sometimes he would have to run from security, but he got the sin he knew wouldn't save him, the sin he sadly wanted, often enough to keep him coming back. In some dorms, he became an amusing, looked-for visitor; just another act on a Friday night, one more outcast doing what he could to try and fix his life, his thumb in the dike.

And perhaps not so surprisingly, some of the women in question liked his nerve, his brazen style. They responded to it, him, because they knew that they were missing out on too much in their own lives. They wanted what they didn't have, hoped to find it with or through him. Or at least a "good" amusement park ride. In any case, there was no shortage of people willing to risk their salvations on any given night.

On especially busy evenings Keith and, most times, Bill would have to walk around campus, find female conversation at the pubs or on the green while they waited for Ron to show. Bill, of course, was not without his own methods, often broke ice with that wide smile of his, questions about the Women's Studies program on campus. Would say he was writing a paper. It was all funny, but very empty at the same time, Keith thought. What were they doing here? Is this what it was all about?

At about three or so, the two of them would usually walk back to the car, their hands in their pockets, and there'd be

Ron, reclined on the hood saying, "Nice night, ain't it boys?" or "Look at all those stars," or "I'm in love this time. . . . I mean it."

The short season began on June 15th, and all three of them started. Ronny was a line drive hitter, could run like a deer. And if his arm was average, his speed seemed to make its strength almost coincidental. Or so it seemed to Keith. But then again he was impressed with everyone. Hitters, pitchers, Bill's arm from behind the plate. He enjoyed the game immensely. It was like a symphony to him: the high, the lows, the arpeggios. How everything could be going along at such a relaxed pace, and then, bam, a hit, every wheel now turning, the crowd itself part of the action.

He had learned to enjoy the pace of the game from Katie, how the radio guys could talk about the breeze coming in from the West or the height of the waves out on the ocean while waiting for the next pitch. There wasn't the constant grunt you got with football. It had real music.

The earlier first round draft choice, Tyrone Peoples, however, didn't seem to share or care much about the game, at least as anything other than an instrument he might use to get what he wanted out of life. He came to training camp late, after bonus squabbles. This surprised no one who saw the obviously angry young black man play. He was a gifted athlete, as quick as Ron, but bigger. And the balls he hit, they were long and graceful arcs which spoke of suspended time, eternity, as one after the other they disappeared high over fences and out into the silence.

But he undercut the beauty himself, offered himself congratulations on each one. "Who-ee. Look at that sucker shine." "One small step for mankind; one large one for my pocketbook."

He put people off immediately, but Keith figured early on that it would be good for Tyrone, the team, if someone could make contact. He introduced himself with his usual extended hand, and Tyrone smiled for a moment, took it. But after a few more patented lines the newest player retreated.

Keith didn't really know what to make of him. Tyrone seemed overly intense in some way, a kettle with the hot lid rattling on the stove. Word was that he had gone to Cal-State Fullerton for a few years, had been a number one pick during each of the subsequent drafts. But it wasn't until he quit the team right before the league championship game that he finally signed. People said he wasn't a team player. Keith couldn't say, but he COULD hear the ticking, figured the best place to be while he waited for the possible explosion was on the other side of the field.

Besides, he had his own impression to make. And make it he did, in the place he felt most comfortable in: his "house," as he called it, that small rectangular piece of real estate outlined, usually on three sides, in chalk. It was the only place in life where he felt he could control things, where he had the final say, and he reveled in that. He loved to hit, feel the feel of good wood. His bat was his tuning fork, and the joy of a note purely hit reverberated through his whole being. It was, he sometimes felt, the only music he would ever need.

It was, as his mother had suggested, the physicality of the whole process that he delighted in. It was living his life, he could feel it, most completely in the present. All of it, life's ups and downs, contained in this little box. "Pandora," he would say, "Come to me."

He made his own somewhat smaller arcs over the outfield fence, hit balls, no more than eight feet off the ground, deep into the gaps. When he stepped up to the plate, everyone stopped talking. Balls, jumping off his bat, gave off a white fizz as they streaked past the infielders. Players would wave their gloves: "Toro, Toro. Olé," they'd yell as if sidestepping snake bites. Rookie league outfield fences audibly rattled as balls smacked hard into and off of them. The batting practice pitcher kept calling him Bob Horner. Keith, though, had his own notions: "Cooperstown," he said. "Call me that."

Socially, he knew he was on a different playing field than the one Ron and Bill spent more of their time on, but that was all right with him. In fact, he felt grateful. For Katie mostly. He did not want to become a slavering hound, didn't want to spend all his time, all his energy chasing women who, in large part, were not worth the catching. And sometimes he chose to stay at home with the comfort his dignity brought him. He'd put in a movie, pop some corn, read a good book.

And when he did go to bars, he found his pleasure usually in nursing his beer, carrying on his conversions at a more leisurely pace. When it was his turn to talk, he'd go on about life, parents, working on cars, about baseball and Northern California, about Katie, fishing.

Ron got impatient with him sometimes, told him that women EXPECTED to be lied to, that it was his job as a young stud to do so. But Keith resisted, kept the interior animal at bay. And the girls in question, it must be said, were for the most part charmed by his approach, or lack of it. They were struck by his calm, his innocence, grateful for the interlude. More than one pressed her scribbled number into his hand with big eyes, asked him to call her sometime.

Eventually, though, all the beer and meat-market perfume, the curves, the pressure, both physical and social, put him, flesh to flesh, against his fallen nature. It was simply a case of spending too many nights too close to an abyss. Despite all my prayers, maneuvers, he fell off. And though it must be said that he felt some relief when it happened—Ron could finally get off his back—some awe too, he was aware that something was slowly changing for him as well.

When he and the women in question eventually rolled apart, when he left their rooms, apartments, it gradually became clear to him, all ego aside, that he had lost something here. His virginity, yes, but something else as well, something less measurable. He felt, he didn't know how to put it, seedier, as if he had just dipped into a murky pool that he hadn't even known existed. He didn't want to get religious or sound like a prude, but things WERE different. He could feel it. Things had changed. He had changed.

It was as if he had been dropped into another world, or, rather, another take on the world, one with less natural hope, one pervaded by a sadness he had not felt so completely before. Here, in this new place, you just went out and got what you wanted, needed. Everybody did. There were no real concerns for abstract ramifications, the other. And no illusions about self either.

Maybe it was the adult world; he didn't know. But he didn't like it. Did things have to be this way? Was there any way back? He didn't know that either, tried to erase what he could of it by going to the park early.

Once there, he'd work harder than ever on his reflexes, stay for an hour after practice, taking grounders, smashed at close range until his bruised body had had enough. Those nights, he'd unpeel his clothing slowly, settle stiffly under his sheets.

It was a planned visit, Katie's, and even though she had told him before he left that she knew and expected that he would probably become more worldly, she could not hide her disappointment.

Usually talkative, she remained quite as they drove back from the airport. Quiet as they pulled over, as they had often done back home when they found a country road or meadow to walk over. Hand in hand, they began to make their way through a field.

"It's good to see you again," she sighed, looking at him and then up at another field, the stars. He couldn't help but notice the tear in her eye, felt a tenderness for her, what he had left behind.

"Hey, what's this? We haven't seen each other for two months, and you come here crying?" He turned her toward him, his hands on both of her shoulders, looked into her welling eyes.

"I'm sorry, Keith. I knew you'd see other people."

"Other people? Where did that come from?"

"Oh, stop. I'm not stupid, you know," she said turning away. "I've talked to your roommates over the phone, remember. . . . Don't you think I've heard those voices before? I've been to college bars. . . . And you, well. . . . I don't know. You're surer of yourself now. Too much so. Your eyes are colder." She turned half way toward him, put her hands to her down-turned face for a moment, patted her own cheeks.

"Forgive me, please," she said, looking quickly at him. "Let's just take our walk, okay. Enjoy the time we've got together. I'll get over it. . . . Your Mom and Dad are doing fine. Did I tell you she's starting a volleyball club in your back yard? . . . Something for the older set. . . her pun. Gin and tonics, volleyball on the side. She's a piece of work, your Mom."

They both laughed, hers with a touch of will, his, a shade muted, as the mention of his Mother brought with it a wave of nostalgia. He sighed, looked out over the field. Katie put her hand on his shoulder. "You miss them, don't you?'

"Yeah, you too," he said, putting his hand over hers. She pulled his arm over her shoulder, put her head on his chest for a good while, and part of her wanted to ask him in when they got back to her motel door. He could see that on her face, the stress, inner struggle as she bit her lower lip, moved her feet.

He kissed her on the lips, and then softly on the forehead just to relieve the pressure the silence had helped create. He suggested she get some sleep. Tomorrow was an off day; there was a lot for them to do.

She told him as he began walking away that she loved him, to which he responded, turning, "Me too." Then he walked away. She read her Bible before she went to bed, cried some, went to sleep.

Things picked up during the rest of the home stand. They spent long hours walking under more leaves, in front of more Victorian porches than she thought possible, making plans for the future under the humid orange streaks of dusky Southern sunsets. They sat out on the shore of some Indian lake she couldn't pronounce, until it was time for her to retire. And since she had to leave the next day, she unwrapped the present she'd bought for him: a Bible. He smiled and took it, spent time going over the fine leather and guilt edges with his hands. He'd read it, he told her, OCCASIONALLY. Both of them laughed.

And if he didn't call himself Christian from that point on, he did make an attempt to steer clear of the bar scene, women, at least during the times he was hitting. And that was most of the time. By August he was leading the league by twenty points. Ron was going pretty well too, but left before the season was over, saying that he could make more bartending in a week than he could in Burlington in a month. $800. Who was kidding whom? He had things to do, faces to see, figured he'd leave while riding high.

He left them both his address, told them to get him some tickets for the show when the time came. Bill, too, started and did okay in the catching department, but his bat never did come around. He would spend two and a half years in A ball before hurting his arm, moving on.

Keith, however, like Tyrone, moved with a bullet up the charts. In the next year he went from lower A at Kingston to upper A in Columbus, leading both teams in hitting. Making $2,200 a month, he saved what he could as Katie, his fiancée by this time, had moved East to join him. He would be twenty next year, she, nineteen. Not old enough to be married they both agreed, but they had to laugh as well. What did sense have to do with any of this? They were young and delighted in each other, in the passion they had to deny. It all came to seem so absurd. They took to late night runs, to Bible reading marathons, Katie to wearing thick sweaters whenever she came over (a coat once), no matter what the temperature. Thankfully, he had air conditioning.

None of it helped much; he'd miss her with pangs during the long bus rides, movie after movie in the VCR overhead: Arnold THE TERMINATOR, Arnold THE PREDATOR, Arnold in TOTAL RECALL. And then Clint, every Jason episode, three movies per ride on long trips.

He got so frustrated with the boredom of it all that he thought of quitting, going back to work with Dad in the shop. But Katie kept after him, encouraging him, worked double shifts as a waitress when he was on the road just to sock away more money. For his part, he saved what he could as well, lived in Goodwill clothes—the players took to calling him "Rags"—hoarded meal money.

And they would need it. They got married before that next season was over. And nine months later, in Canton, a baby girl, Ruth, moved into the photographs with all her attendant baggage: rattles, wiggly worms, water-filled teething bears.

With another mouth to feed, Keith redoubled his efforts, played winter ball in Puerto Rico. He and Katie and Ruth, living in Carolina, putting up with a bland apartment to save money, lush palm garden/patio, the ocean notwithstanding. They scraped by with her high school Spanish, friendly smiles, and a check that had them eating more rice and beans than the apartment could on some nights stand.

Still, it seemed to him that they were pretty well off, at least compared to how the poor had to live, the old shacks thrown up out on the plush green countryside just outside of the city. He heard these people had been evicted by the government from low-cost housing units. Something about the gentrification of neighborhoods. Their cows lived better than they did, munching on all that rich tropical foliage while the small gray thrown-together houses, like all the old midwestern barns he'd seen during bus rides, leaned toward collapse.

It bothered him, the injustice of it all. He'd punch his fist into an absurdly manicured blue glove every day, accept the money they gave him, go shopping with Katie to malls only people like them could afford. They were tourists, he thought, perhaps in the bigger picture too, living on the top of the food chain, cruising through life, sampling what it offered them along the way: Old San Juan, out-of-the-way eateries, coral and blue waters.

What kind of life was this anyway? Would it ever demand anything substantial from him, or could he just go on this way, picking the flowers in this field until his life was over?

Katie was undaunted by these considerations though. They worked hard for their meager wages; they deserved what they got. And they would deserve the bigger money, too, when it came. Why apologize for what he should be proud about, for what God, as she knew Him, blessed them with? She didn't understand that part of Keith, but stood right by him through all those tough early years, leaning with him in harness, leaning on him if she felt she had to, trying to help make their dreams physical.

It wasn't that she didn't have her doubts; it was just that, for her, those more pertinent questions lived too close to home for her to allow them any sway. She disliked being at the park on cold early May days, Baby Ruthie next to her, taking refuge behind the plexiglassed ground level lounge window at Thurman Munson Stadium. She wondered if it would all pay off, would try to keep a good face on the effort, lift Ruthie up, get her to wave at slumping Daddy as he rubbed the pine tar rag into the grain of his suddenly lifeless bat handle.

The whole scene seemed so childish to her sometimes. The minor leagues with its avalanche of promotions: one lucky fan picked every night, awarded a free haircut, or grown women, with shovels after a game, digging up the infield in their mad search for a hidden ring. She hated the local cuisine specials. It was barbecue in North Carolina, perogis here. She disliked the p.a. announcers with their corny jokes, disliked each "Town of Friendly People."

Here they were, after all, a couple of adults with child, trying to wade through minor league cities, trying to "play" with the big boys, at a game, for sweet Jesus' sake. What kind of existence was this for grown-up people really, she wondered? What would they do if he ever got hurt and couldn't play any more? Shouldn't he be preparing for something that had more long-haul possibilities?

It gnawed at her as she looked around in the loge. Was this the life she had pictured for herself three years ago: the stained industrial carpet, the jugs of Minnehaha water in the corner beneath the bolted-in hospital TV, the dirty microwave and mounds of Bit-O-Honey candy bars next to it? There were lamps with tacky baseball bats, cheap helmets for stands, bad couches; there were pictures of past teams—very few of those players now in the big leagues— a picture of Thurman fat Munson on the wall as well.

No, sometimes she hated it.

And to top it all off, Keith got only one or two off days per month. Despite the fact that their season was shorter than the mother club's, they still played 141 games between April 6th and September 4th. She grew weary of taking Ruth to the park on all those afternoons alone, swinging her on the same old swings, chumming up with other women whom she really didn't care much for when their husbands were out of town.

She got tired of sitting home all by herself during all the eastern trips, the Salisbury steak TV dinners on her lap, the apartment meagerly furnished, questionable noises on the street, in the halls, flimsy locks, Ruthie rustling in a used crib. She hoped, prayed hard, with many tears, for a better life.

And, like so much, in time it came. Keith got invited to spring training in January. And though most of the players there were outwardly friendly enough, they spoke to him as they had probably spoken to rookies each year since Abner Doubleday: encouraging, in an impersonal way, giving the occasional tip about what went on around the bag at this level.

He played the role, stayed after school, tried to stay out of everybody's way. This was what he had been waiting for since high school, but he felt a great distaste for the whole process now that he was involved in it as well. It was like a country club that he couldn't get into. He didn't know the handshake. He was not welcome, or so it seemed to him. He was the little boy, patted on the head, sent off to school.

So he did what he always did when things went against him. He remembered the horse in ANIMAL FARM from English class. "I will work harder." Most of the irony aside, he would just have to make things happen.

He used it, his rage to hit .430, took chances on the bases. And it got him recognized. Reporters began writing stories about him, kids were happy to get his autograph, players remembered his name. But he wasn't where he wanted to be yet. He wasn't one of them. He would have to push harder, keep the pose, make deference/anger a way of life; he put apples on the manager's desk for a few days, then a pineapple, then a bushel of corn.

His attempts paid off. To his joy, he became the butt of a practical joke. Even if the other players didn't know as much, they had given him identity. He had a foot in the door. Someone had placed a huge mound of cow dung in front of his locker, most of his equipment underneath it, shoes sticking out the sides like his ears beneath the hat.

He responded to the inattentive players milling about in a heart-broken tone, biting his finger: "I feel so used." But as he went outside he couldn't contain his glee. Jumping into his car, he raced to a store and bought a straw hat, some bib overalls, wheeled in a groundskeeper's barrow and a shovel, cleaned it up.

But this game wasn't over yet, he decided. It couldn't be. Three and five days later, in his mad zeal to make a permanent impression, he upped the ante, called in bomb threats. The players were grateful, if shocked, and he found four packages of new golf balls in his locker on the sixth day. Someone had included the note, "And on the seventh day He rested."

And the players weren't the only ones now bringing the handshake. In the papers, and in person, the brass talked of keeping him with the big club when they headed north. He kept his pose. Katie figured it was a sure thing, what with how well he was doing. But it was not to be, and she suffered most with the demotion. He would start the regular season in Triple A.

The organization had opted to go the more conservative route, stay with steady experience. He was disappointed, if not surprised and told himself that, after all, he had acquitted himself well, and, well, what could be done about THEIR decisions anyway. The only place he had any control after all was between that chalk.

But it affected him. His wife could tell. He started talking to himself as they slowly packed their bags, the soup bones he used to hone his bats from the fridge. He'd just have to keep after it, he told himself, take extra fielding, hitting. Don't worry. He'd get there, and soon.

But then high Providence moved. The incumbent, John Sullivan, fractured an ankle in a minor car accident. He would be out for two months. Katie reacted initially with jubilation, she and little Ruthie dancing on the living room rug.

But then it hit her. Sullivan's family. Should they send a card?

"One man's ceiling is another man's floor," said Keith, sanding a bat, examining the grain carefully.

In the end she decided that they should pray the Lord would bless the Sullivan family—maybe get him traded. (They both laughed.) Katie thanked God later that night in bed, tears running down her face. Finally, they would get their chance.

This was the opportunity he had been waiting for, and when it came, Keith seized that day as if there would be no other. He had to make these two months count, and decided to stay aggressive, but quietly so this time. He would not draw any undue attention to himself outside of what he could produce with his bat, his glove. He would show up and do what they asked him to. He would stick his face in a blender.

He sent Ron and Bill some opening day tickets, asked his elders in the craft for advice at every turn, about every pitcher, every defensive situation. He ran the bases, as Katie put it, as if his pants were on fire. And if he made mistakes, he never made the same ones twice. Freize beamed, the fans cheered. He had talent, chin, and they were winning. You could hit this guy in the head with a fastball, and he'd sprint down to first, crowd the plate a little more at the next at bat, try to take another one for the team.

He was a cheerleader as well, pushed hard to win. And the press took up his cause, called him Gonzo until a writer heard Ruthie, coming as close as she could to that, call him "Beto."

And Beto stayed, was still there in September, the team in third place. Katie was buoyed by his Rookie-of-the-Year performance, suggested that they consider leasing a bigger place.

It was an exhilarating ride for both of them, but like any job, it began to age with time. Within a few years, though his success didn't, the glitter for Keith had for the most part lost its allure. Tyrone was named Rookie of the Year two seasons on, hit around a crowded batting cage. And Keith didn't mind, was glad for him in fact, gave him whatever tips he could.

As for his own approach, Keith found that more and more often now, though he still liked the game a great deal, he was growing tired of the whole scene. But the pay was so good; he just kept showing up, punching the clock, producing. And if through the years his numbers, both pay-wise and statistically, always good, now put him in the highest level of players at his position, he became aware as well that he was a commodity here, counted on and then forgotten.

He still enjoyed the game, his teammates, but it had gotten to be a business, just the thing that he did. So he took what it gave him, lived there behind the mask of professionalism, went home when his day was done. And if that mask proved too heavy to lift on some days, even for a "star," if it proved a barrier to any real communication, human interaction, at least it provided him, ironically, with some solitude. All he could get in the emptiness.

He had to deal with what his position had done to him and to other people. For whomever he met during the season, he never met. They were a sea of corporate faces, talking heads, little kids, every one of them. The whole dreary enterprise made him miss the homestead: Mom's bad soup, jokes, fishing trips with Dad and his friends, wet sleeping bags, running from bears.

Katie, though, was in her element. She seemed to truly blossom under the lights of celebrity. On bad days Keith tried to find his consolation there. The years would take care of themselves. He had a lovely family. Besides, whom was he kidding? There were people out there on the dole, on unemployment lines with mouths to feed. He owned a huge boat, could go golfing five days a week, all because he could hit a slightly bigger ball. What was the problem? Go figure, he'd say to himself. No, go chase— young man. Go chase. And he did.

But complacency never lasts. Though bodies, as physics tells us, tend to rest if not moved upon, they can never stay there either. What comes is further dissolution, or change, conversion. Though sometimes one can't immediately tell the difference.

And late one season, if you listened closely, on another plane, you could hear the stone axis begin to turn. The couple found out, belatedly, that Katie was two months pregnant. She wasn't sure at first that she wanted another child just then, but Keith's excitement won her over soon enough.

They bought a huge five bedroom suburban house with a large white curved banistered stairwell near the front double doors, sparkling linoleum beneath. There were high shaft windows on the south side of the house, a complete workout room, pool table, swimming pool, and a three car garage. They put on a maid and rented a landscaper to take care of their five-acre lawn. Keith bought Katie a red BMW and put up a basketball hoop.

And Katie was happy. You could hear her sigh some mornings, sitting in the sunny breakfast room out back, her Bible on her lap, watching the birds in their feeders, the squirrels as they leaped tree to tree in high firs. At last. They had arrived. This felt like home: the water twinkling in the pool, the fresh needled air, the sound of Ruthie's running feet on the best floors their money could buy.

And things only got better. They found good neighbor friends on both sides, would invite them over for barbecue, swimming parties. As it turned out, both couples belonged to the same Assembly of God Church, invited Katie and Keith to join them. It was, to her way of thinking, all finally coming together. The years in the desert were over. This was Canaan.

The Church was holy, Bible-believing, and both of them immediately took to it. It was spirit-filled, exuded a sense of community, family. And if some part of Keith had trouble with this local church's rather comfortable idea of community action: coming in a phalanx of vans to the inner city every weekend to help teach Sunday school, distribute food to the needy, he also liked them as people. They seemed accessible, meek even. (So many of them, in one way or another, expressing heartfelt gratitude for what the Lord had done in their lives.)

They welcomed him, his whole family, with open arms, and he welcomed that, the chance to get some distance between himself and his public image.

Katie chirped like a bright bird around the house. She stayed after the maid, ran a very tight ship, insisted on new towels and new sheets every day. She delighted in trying new decorating ideas, wall papers, busts and pictures, was thrilled to have her home featured in OHIO HOMES AND GARDENS.

There were never any spots on the bathroom mirrors, any dirt that the dirt-vac couldn't pick up with a quick and happy swipe. All Ruthie's toys were in convenient stacked plastic wire bins; everyone's clothes were clean. Too clean, Keith sometimes felt.

It was such a tight ship, in fact, that he felt he could hear it squeak. The sunny snow-white fabric softener days which beamed like promises kept began to depress him. He missed the messiness he had grown up with, the down home quality of old flapping screens, flaking paint. He felt like a boarder in his own house, like he had to walk on eggshells, clean the soles of his shoes as he moved from room to room. He missed his Dad, the joyful streak of grease across his forehead, the two of them under the hood some nights, talking women or cars. He missed his Mother, forever after both of them for one thing or another.

His life, he began to feel, like the church he belonged to, all seemed to express Katie's effort to sanitize their existence. He wondered, were they that dirty? Katie, Katie, this woman he loved. Katie, with a vengeance.

What a weird life theirs was! He was grateful for what she'd given to him, and he still hoped their two ways might blend before too long, that they might become one in ways he had grown up expecting: parents beginning to look alike, each couple's house, with its comfortable smell. Not too much, of course, not offensive, just a down-home whiff of years spent together, of the children produced, of their friends and quarrels.

But they'd been married for six years now. He wondered if any of that was forthcoming. She was so sure of herself, an iron maiden despite her goodness. Probably she would never change, would just outlive him, erase any odors that remained, keep new flowers on his grave.

He had long admired her faith life, but even when these Christians were depressed, they looked like they were going full speed ahead to him, or took pains to appear so. They talked of "faithing it." He didn't know what to make of the whole thing. He liked them for the most part, but on some days he felt a strong sense of rebellion when he was with them. Maybe it was some devil harassing him, as the preacher had talked about. He didn't know, tried to let go of the resentment when it came and kept busy pounding the weights, working out with some guys who'd come over during that winter.

Besides, there was Ruthie to spend time with. There were sled rides, igloos to build, ice balls to make. It wasn't such a bad life.

Both he and Katie enjoyed his parents. They looked forward to letters. Her parents, though, were another story. They were too proud, demanding for him, and he disliked them. They had some money, had criticized her for years for going around with an athlete until he had made it. Then Dad got friendly, though it was clear he considered Keith in some way "new money"—an odd notion, Keith decided, considering the fact that the old boy didn't really have enough to qualify as "old." Katie had tried to smooth Keith's feathers, but he resented them and what he saw as their glass cage. So stops were always brief, to Katie's dismay, when they were in the neighborhood. The two of them, Keith and Katie, like most couples, dealt with their problems as they came up, in most cases allowing time, a let-it-go attitude, to do the healing.

Things had been rolling along on mostly even tracks for some time. Since both were basically optimistic people and liked to keep busy, they found it pretty easy to look at the sunny side of things whatever their mutual peeves. There was joy and laughter, fat ankles and backaches as the Mrs. found herself rounding, moreso than last time it seemed to her, out of shape.

Dad and Ruthie would help out whenever they could: provide extra pillows for Mom's back, help her in and out of the car. He even put on a cook for awhile. There were Sesame Street movies, and then when Ruth was asleep, romantic comedies. And the machine might have continued clattering, huffing right along were it not for an eventful visit that January.

Katie, having pushed for years, finally got a subdued Julia to consent; she would go with them to church on Sunday. And though it seemed odd to Keith to see his Mother in a pill box hat, he went with it. She was always on her own wave length. Mom, at church! Why not, he said to himself. Maybe there ARE miracles after all. That made him smile, at least early on.

About halfway through the quest speaker's rehearsed tears and alleluias, though, he saw something that shook him. His mother's shoulders. They were softly shaking, up and down. Was she? No, she couldn't be. But she was. Crying!

At first he was shocked, puzzled. And he might have gotten over it, but the people around her could hear as well. Before he could even figure out how to handle the situation, everyone surrounding her laid hands on Julia's head and shoulders, asked Jesus to take her by the hand, heal her.

But the tears, to Keith's consternation, did not subside, at least not initially. They increased in volume. Keith lay his hand on her too, though he didn't know how to pray, what to say. He was concerned about his Mother, annoyed at the preacher for continuing with his harangue.

These initial reactions, to his satisfaction, began to fade. He lifted up his metaphorical heart to God, wanted Him to help her. But then another wave of feelings swamped him, different ones. Anger at first. He didn't like her expressing a need so publicly. What was she trying to do? After all, this WAS his church. He was well-known here, though everyone in the congregation had always taken pains to keep the situation normal. (And as he thought these things, he realized that his feelings about the place were mixed. On the one hand, he wanted to feel as if he were just one of the crowd, but on the other, he appreciated the hand too heartily given, the cracks in timid newly-met voices. He had grown used to it, now felt guilty over that fact that he'd obviously, unconsciously, been reveling in it. Stupid pride. And wouldn't he know it, it was his Mother who showed it to him.)

And then there was another wave of emotion. More anger, this time solely at her. She always had to be the center of things. She just couldn't give him his space. He disliked her for what she was doing, but soon began to dislike himself, too, for his insensitivity.

Julia, however, was not conscious of his feelings. She seemed to respond positively to all the attention she was getting, lit up with tongues and joyful tears as the prayer portion of the service ended. She began hugging everyone around her, praising Jesus, holding her hat to keep in on. Everyone was delighted for her.

Everyone except for Keith. He felt stress in his face and couldn't wait for the amenities to end so he could leave that place.

His mother was of course oblivious to that feeling as well. He could see that. It was her moment, he decided sneeringly, and as far as she was concerned she needed the strokes. How quickly her hands were on other people's arms, how quickly she laughed with people she didn't even know. It all struck him as being so typical of her. Julia the avenger, inflicting herself on all she surveyed.

This time it was Jesus. He had touched her she said, changed her. She'd seen him as people prayed; He held her and told her that He loved her, that she could lean on Him. And the tears, tongues. Where had she learned those he wondered? It couldn't have been acting classes; she never needed them before.

Finally the "show" just got to be too much for him. He cut her off by abruptly telling her and Katie in front of "a nice young couple" that it was time to get back. If they wanted a ride home they could come. Julia laughed and waved him away, told him that he was funny. The Lord would take care of them; they could get a ride with someone else.

"Oh no you're not. You're embarrassing the hell out of me. Now come on," he said loudly, jerking her along by her elbow.

"I hope so," Julia said, still trying to keep her hat on. Katie was shocked at his behavior, but Julia, undaunted, got in final waves, blew a few final dramatic kisses to further embarrass her son. "I'm being dragged to the lions!"

Katie gave the eye to her husband as they approached the car, hugged her mother-in-law in a sustained way once they'd gotten near the door. It was one of those hard hugs, the kind that actually has both people shaking a little as they do so. Taking out a tissue, she wiped away a few of Julia's tears and took her by the elbow, pregnant though she was, helped her other mother into the back seat. "Praise God, Mom," she said, hugging her again as the older woman settled into her seat. As they buckled themselves in, she wiped away a tear from her own eye, socked her calming husband on his arm, "Watch out, pagan. You might be next."

At home, amid more hugging, laughing, occasional scripture consultation, Julia and Katie got down to the business of making lunch. They rummaged through the fine white cupboards, gold-leafed, finding joy, jokes in the pasta, cans of soup.

"Blessed are the soup makers," said Julia. "For they shall find their peas."

"Mrs. Wells!" responded Katie, her look expressing both shock and humor.

"Oh, lighten up, Katie. We ARE loved you know. In the immortal words of Pigwig: 'I'm so-o-o-o hap-py," she said, raising her skirt a little bit with both hands, spinning. "'You'll not mind if I say 'it-ti-dy, tid-i-ty? I've forgotten some of the words.'"

"Julia, what ARE you talking about?"

"Reader's Theater. For pre-schoolers. . . Do you have any mayonnaise," she asked, head in the refrigerator? "The Kingdom of heaven is like a bologna sandwich," she continued, then peeked out. "Finish, please."

"I don't know. . . because the world understands it not. . . . I'm not very good at this. Praise God."

"Oh, you're good enough. . . . How's about some nice sliced cantaloupe? A bowl of sherbet, just to celebrate?"

"Great. So you've been reading your Bible? When did all this start?"

"About four years ago." They both laughed. "But more seriously, last summer. I had too much space to fill, you know. . . . Heck, you can't talk to yourself around the dinner table." Katie shook her head "yes" as her mother-in-law continued. "I used to watch this guy on t.v. just for fun. He'd spend half his program time asking for donations; I timed him once. He had a good thing going, too, offering prayer cloths, spinning his prayer wheel. He even offered bowling balls with "I love Jesus" stenciled across it for God's sake. . . . He'd take to crying. I thought he was the biggest huckster I'd ever seen. . . . The whole thing seemed like an unintentional parody, you know? I mean the guy wore a cheap toupee. . . . the thing must've weighed four pounds. . . . It was funny. But I was feeling lonely, too, empty. The thing got to me on some level. At first I thought it was just my mood, that I'd get over it. But I found myself watching it over and over, actually looking forward to it! Finally, I figured, what the heck, I'd take you up on your offer, see if I was losing my mind. . . . And you know what?"

"Yes, I know," her daughter-in-law said, playfully touching her arm. "Praise God. So a TV Evangelist got you, huh? That's funny. Well, weirder things have happened."

"I guess. I just never took the time to work my way through it all, you know. As a mother I was busy with Keith and his Father, but that odd preacher got me wondering. Was life supposed to feel so empty? Was I supposed to be walking around with this hole inside? . . . Anyway one of the women in my volleyball club began giving me tracts, so I started reading the Bible more seriously, I mean, what did I have to lose, right?'

"Your burden!"

"Amen. And it feels gone. Isn't that amazing. 'Ain't God good,' as that preacher used to say?" At this point she imitated some of the TV evangelist's movements, slapped Katie on the forehead. They both laughed, then took to the preparations.

Katie stopped after a moment, unlatched the winter window. "Smell those trees—just for a minute." And with a little more laughter, reacting to the cold, she threw some bread out the window.

Julia watched the birds take to it. "Blessed are the breadmakers."

"For theirs is the kingdom of leaven," Katie said. They both approved.

"Lettuce rejoice."

The sun shone on the snow outside the play room window; the fir trees were caked in the stuff, and as cold winds bobbed the limbs shelves of it dropped down only to dissipate in a swirl of breezes. It reminded Keith of the first time he saw snow. The tingling of his nose, how you could plow through it with your feet. He and Katie had tried to unsuccessfully build a snowman. (The snow was too cold.)

He heard them downstairs laughing. It was like he wasn't even there. So he went over to where Ruthie and a neighbor girl were playing with their Barbie dolls, ran his fingers through her hair, kissed her on the forehead. She was surprised at this display of emotion in front of her friend, but she looked up at him too, big-eyed. Something was up.

He moved away and stood closer to the window, wondered what was happening to his life. Things used to be so regular and manageable, so up front. They were a team and pulled together. But now there were twists and turns, all of it well beyond him. And how much of this was his anyway really? Ruthie would eventually grow up and get married; his playing days would be history soon enough. And what would he do then? Do the baseball card circuit? Talk radio? There didn't seem to be any more hills for him. All of it would be decline. Most of it, if he was lucky, graceful. Eventually he would get old and bent, a strange woman across the room who'd be singing songs to Jesus, her hands raised, doing silly dances while he puttered around and looked for something to do.

His Mother came quietly into the room. She stood next to him for a good while, looking out of the same window before she spoke. He shouldn't be mad. She'd finally found what she was after. She now knew Jesus and was changed. That was a great miracle. He should be happy for her.

He didn't want to hear it, though, felt confirmed in his reservations as she began to slowly pour her heart out to him. With small creaking sounds he could hear it open.

She began to, as she put it, "share": how distant Dad had become these last few years, how she'd felt like a failure her whole life, accomplishing nothing, no matter how much of the load she had to carry. She said she felt exhilarated and enthusiastic for the first time in decades, was profoundly grateful. He should try it.

She went on and on, about a possible art career, something she'd always wanted to do, about traveling, ministering to women with marital problems. Maybe she could start a hotline, get an 800 number? She'd need a wheel for the pottery, of course. Say, maybe she could find a cheap one here. California was so trendy. They were sure to be more expensive out there.

It made him nauseous as it seemed an awfully sudden spate of revelations, solutions. What about the spelling and reading bees back home that she'd begun to orchestrate? What about the mature set's volley ball games out back, the accompanying gin and tonics? His mother just laughed. "The cries of a desperate woman!" She might still do some of that, but she was a new creature now too. Maybe she might take some time and get away, she mused, spend some time apart from his father. Who knows, it might help their marriage.

She did look sunny and happy, unencumbered, but he wondered. Could this be her own mother all over again? It seemed wrong to him for some reason. The too easy flick of a switch. "I once was lost, but now I'm special" routine. Did she need to be the center THAT badly? And what would be next, an encounter with aliens, the Moonies? He could just see her, outside the White House, taking up the cause of an endangered species of slugs.

When she left the next week, she seemed to take everything but his anger with her. He and Katie began to drift farther and farther apart as weeks passed. He noticed her every flaw, attributed each to her faith in the God she created, or to her up-bringing, or to her skewed personality. And bitter and cynical though his attitude certainly was, what he found WAS there. She, like all of God's physical creatures, was flawed. It ran as deep as she was, and nothing could have changed that. But what he didn't see, what people seldom do, was that it was her salvation as well. She lived for a mercy that sustained them, that neither one of them could see.

And his blindness worked both ways. Which human, after all, does not deserve judgment? Which, if he were truly honest with himself, would still cry out that he was worthy of a better fate, a healthier mate?

But those answers lie in the provinces of humility, a province whose borders he had not yet caught sight of.

And when the letter finally came, from Hawaii, pictures of his mother in a hoop skirt, a native next to her teaching her how to dance, he lost all hope, told Katie he wanted to sell the house. There were arguments, dishes thrown.

Katie, who was six months pregnant at the time, would cry at the drop of a hormone anyway. So the fights began to come on a regular basis.

Ruthie began to sulk, stay in her room, and lose weight. They were on the verge of a split when their gynecologist told them that Katie needed an extra ultrasound. "Polyhydramnios," was the reason he gave, an excess of amniotic fluid. Also there was a "double-bubble."

He sent Katie and her tests to a university hospital, told them not to worry. Doctors there did an amniocentesis and infant heart sonograms. There was little doubt by the time the tests were completed. The baby had Down's Syndrome, duodenal atresia, a bad heart. It would need operations after it was born, if, indeed, it were to be born.

The woman doctor asked Katie if she were Catholic. When Katie waved off the possibility, the woman suggested that she might consider the quality of life question, society, in her decision. What kind of life could it lead given all these problems? Would it be wise to ask the state to assume adult care after they, as parents, were out of the picture? Even though the issue was six months old at that point, abortion WAS a legal option, or if the prospect of that was too much for her, she could have it and they could do a partial birth and charitably donate the organs to the hospital. They both were young after all. There would be many more opportunities to get it right.

Catching the anger on Katie's face, the doctor went on to say that she felt it was her professional duty to let patients know all the available options. She wasn't advocating anything.

Katie paused, then spoke very slowly. Did the doctor think Catholics had a monopoly on pro-life issues? Just who did she think she was, anyway, to so callously reduce a person to an "issue"? Was that her idea of bedside manner? Or was she just seriously stunted emotionally? Why didn't she just keep her stupidity to herself and do what she was put on to do, deliver the baby. Katie reminded her as well that she knew several of the hospital's trustees and that, if the doctor didn't make an immediate apology, she would complain vigorously about her attitude.

The woman began to flush, was going to respond, but thought the better of it. She gathered herself, turned and walked crisply out of the room.

The birth, as the new doctor suggested it would, came early. Keith had to miss some spring training to be there, but he reveled in the process. He squeezed Katie's hand during delivery and got her to blow as she should through the latter stages. Her one eyelid turned inside out for a time as her moods, levels of pain swung: at times she looked to him for help, at other times, suspicion was all that he saw. But they hung in, the both of them. He, supporting, and she, as if on a mission, pushing with such vigor that they would later find out she tore some tissue.

Would the little guy be okay they both wondered? How much will to live would he have left, after having continuously vomited every thing he swallowed in the womb?

Their fears were, almost immediately, put to rest. Once outside the womb, the little boy, after a few healthy screams, tried to breathe in his first fallen air through his nose and couldn't. It was clogged. Both Keith and the nurse next to him, for the briefest of seconds, held their breaths.

But the boy was a true Wells, after all, and responded to his first hurdle by immediately blowing the cheesy material some ten feet across the room, all its infant fury behind it. And the baby's will to live, rage, only increased as residents took him to an adjoining room to get some NG feeds in. His cry had such volume that newcomers in the birth room wondered what he was so mad at.

The happy parents hoped to take the baby home immediately after the first operation, but the hospital delayed, wanted to monitor the badly-formed heart. As it turned out, the baby needed a pulmonary banding until an open heart operation could be done at the one year mark, when he would be stronger and weighed about twenty pounds.

The observation period lasted another month. Every time his parents wanted to hold him, they had to lift him from his incubator, sort through all the wires and tubes: navel, chest, back, head, the ET toe light, each, it seemed, binding the little guy in a fine medical filigree.

The nurses were kind enough, but despite all their shift meetings they never seemed to be able to agree on what was going on, on what had been done, on what was to be done. All of this only served to further aggravate Katie, who, sometimes feeling like a defective mother, saved her milk, frozen, in little bags.

After they finally got him home, it was touch and go for awhile. Katie tried to hang in there, but it was a struggle. On some days she really sank. She'd get depressed as she nursed, would cry her way through what she could do of it. Keith, flying in whenever he could, would warm up some formula and take the baby from her to finish the job. He'd walk him around the house and sing "Take me out to the Ball Game" to Tommy until he fell to sleep. And then he'd see to Katie, tuck her in, get her some hot soup. The whole thing, though sad, had energized him in some subtle way, humanized him. All any of them could do in life was make the best of it, he figured. All they could do was try.

Julia unexpectedly showed up one weekend, from Acapulco, to try and help. All tanned and smiling, bracelets jangling on her wrists, her flowered dress, short tinted hair, she brought with her an insufferable good will. She immediately threw open the curtains in Katie's room, told her they were going shopping. Keith was grateful, wanted to ring her neck.

But it worked, whatever it was she brought: her good will, her enthusiasm. And soon enough just the two of them, surrounded by bouquets of flowers and opened curtains, Tommy squalling intermittently in the crib Julia rocked next to them, were talking excitedly about healing ministries. Julia had planned the whole itinerary, opened maps, one next to the other on the bed between them.

As the cassette of loud religious songs ended, Keith could, through the door, hear Julia talk about seven healers who were going to appear in the state within the next few weeks. The two of them could rent a plane and make them all if they planned it just right, hustled a bit. Julia had the locations marked in magic marker yellow, the flight paths in blue, time tables in red.

Keith stormed in, objected vigorously. He didn't want them taking Ruthie and little Tom around to a bunch of quacks. It might have long-term effects. They weren't going to do it, forget it. What they needed around their house was some calm acceptance, some normalcy.

Julia shooed him away. "Oh, he just needs some time alone. Aren't you due for one of those roads trips or something? We've got some work to do here." Then she went back, picked up on their conversation as if they'd never been interrupted. Keith felt angry at the both of them, felt like a rookie again, on the outs with no way to get into the club.

He clenched his fists in anger, verging on violence, but knew aggressive behavior wouldn't help here. So he rocked, turned, and went out to the kitchen. What could he do to stop this? He didn't know. Finally, to clear his head he splashed some cold water on his face from the kitchen sink, tried to figure out how to bring some sanity back into the house. It WAS his house, wasn't it? What did they need her coming in here for, disrupting the healing process with fantasy?

Finally, after pacing back and forth, listening to laughter from the other room, he panicked. He took Ruth and rushed out the door. And after driving around the ballpark for awhile, he stopped and went in. With Ruthie testing echoes from the pitcher's mound, he walked the ledge of grass between infield and outfield and wondered what to do with his life. Its borders kept him in, kept him from enjoying any of it. Or much of it. He looked at his daughter, the stands.

They would be filled tomorrow. People would expect him to perform as if he had no other life. Just like his wife, they would expect him to play the trained seal. Carry our lives for us. Just for three hours. Take it from our shoulders. And then they'd go home in a thousand directions to what they considered their homes.

But how much of that was real? Their homes didn't belong to them, in financial or ultimate terms, anymore than his did. Their lives, like his, if they were lucky, would go on, filled with trivia and distraction. What WAS real? He wanted to know. Certainly not his life, not the way he was living it, not the way it was being lived for him. The whole thing became too much. And in a fit of bitterness, anger, he took his daughter to the airport.

They touched down in Miami that evening where the two of them put up in the hotel Ruthie liked best, the one with the most sparkly lights on the outside. He ordered some Barney tapes and drank champagne as the two of them watched, ate lobster and grapes. He hated his life.

He rented a car the next day. They bought silly hats, two pair of the fanciest set of binoculars he could find, and headed for the tall grass of the Everglades. Paging slowly through bird and flower books he had just purchased, the two of them looked for and at the flora and the fauna, walked the elevated wooden bridges. At one point they had to take a wide loop around two small alligators which were sunning themselves on the asphalt walk.

It was peaceful there, as he had hoped it would be. He watched Ruthie skip along the walks in her sunglasses, and his heart sank. She was no longer the baby girl he remembered. When she squealed with delight at the alligators she sounded more like an teenager than anything else. It made him sad. No flight in the world could save him from its turning.

After a few hours the fun was over. Though he had enough money to stay away indefinitely, he did not have the resolve. There was nothing out here for him but tall grass. He was a boat out on no water, in the middle of nothing, with nothing to moor him or give him direction. Duty, the anchor of an empty man, he thought, called. It was not much, but it WAS something.

But as he got back to the hotel he balked. He didn't want to go back, at least not yet. So he drove around until Ruthie fell asleep, pulled out Ron's number. And as he headed over he thought of the good old days. Burlington and the bull's eye over the right center field fence. Hit it and you got a grand. Of course none of them ever did. Keith, though, had won two monthly team pools by getting closest to it.

Ron was surprised to hear from him. Didn't he have a game to go to? An all-points would be out tomorrow, no? But he knew, too, before he opened the door that Keith would not have come this far out of his way had there not been a serious problem, so he took pains to let his friend know beneath the jibes that he was there for him.

What was up, family problems, hitting problems? At the mention of that, Ron got up and started demonstrating his long neglected stance with a bat he still had from those Burlington days, talked humorously about the great hits he'd gotten. He slapped his back thigh, emphasized hip rotation, where it all starts. Keith laughed, and then laughed again as he enjoyed Ron's look of dumb amazement. ("What?")

Yes, Keith confided. It was his religious wife. Ron listened without looking directly at him, his attention focused on the nicks in the bat. He gave him what he could, told Keith that he had divorced his own wife the year before, but that had only helped him. That harness was beat. They wanted different things.

He said he sometimes wondered if marriage was humanly possible, but joked right after saying that's what everybody says after their first marriage. On the other hand, though, he wasn't in a big hurry to find out what everybody said after their second either.

For him now, he said, it was his kids: his family. That was his first priority. He got them on weekends—Keith should see little Jeffrey's swing, smooth as a baby's butt. Ron said he wouldn't let anything get in the way of that. His little girl was in ballet. He laughed about showing up for recitals and said that it was just one of those things you had to tough out. Work took second place with him any more.

Ron was regional director of sales for an appliance company and was doing well despite the fact that his townhouse looked like a better version of the apartment they had shared all those years ago. "Who does the cooking?" Keith asked.

"The maid," Ron said, joking. "A different one every week." And then as he warmed up some left over breaded veal for his guest, some fried potatoes, Ruthie still out, he talked about his brother whom he had been estranged from for many years. Psychological problems. Ron said he made it a point to take him to ballgames and bars to try to help him get on an even keel. He talked about his sister, a school teacher in DesMoines. The three of them try to get over to the folks' place three or four times a year.

What counts for you, he said, that's the question. Family, well blood anyway, was where it was at for him. He confided that he'd even taken in a few seminars to hone his interpersonal skills. What would Cassano have made of that he paused to wonder?

After they ate and piled the dishes in the sink, Ron told Keith about a woman friend who would be happy to sit for Ruthie. Maybe the two of them could prowl through the jungle, do a few fern bars.

On the sparsely crowded plane Ruthie felt free to roam around once they were safely in the sky, talk to the stewardesses, look through circled fingers at other passengers. She took to playing hide-and-seek with a guy across the aisle wearing what appeared to her to be a funny brown dress. The guy, some kind of monk apparently, didn't seem to mind much, so Keith let it go. He was too troubled to think much about it early on. Where was his marriage going anyway? Was it worth saving, and if so, what did he have to do to save it? What would he have to give up? And what about all this religious crap anyway? His wife, his mother, they all seemed like marionettes to him. Would he have to submit to strings to keep his babes?

He had no answers, tried to nap. Ruthie eventually roused him by showing him a string of beads a man had given her. Then it hit him with a start. All the stuff he'd been hearing about on the news: about priests. This guy might be dangerous. Still half asleep, he surprised his daughter by how violently he grabbed her, pulled her toward him.

Seeing her chin begin to tremble and the shocked countenance of the middle aged man, Keith decided that what he really needed to do here was to calm down. He rubbed his face with both hands and apologized to his daughter, kissed her on the top of her head. They were on a plane, after all; what could this guy, fifteen years older and pudgy, do?

"I hope she's not bothering you?"

"Oh no," the monk laughed. "A charming child. Curious though. Aren't you?" he asked her, plucking and holding what might be her nose between his thumb and forefinger. Then he looked at Keith. "That's the hardest thing for us, you know? Family. . . . Not libido, though that gets the headlines. The thought of leaving no one behind," he said with a trace of sadness in his voice.

"Well, forget it. She's mine," Keith said, trying to pick the guy up.

"I have four dollars."

"John Belushi, right? What was it? . . . The BLUES BROTHERS!" Keith and the robed man laughed as they remembered.

They got on, started talking about what they did and where they were coming from. The priest had just come back from some apparition sight in Croatia. As he explained it all to Keith, Keith thought of his wife, her faith.

What could he do about his whole situation, he asked? "Pray," the priest said. Fast, if he could do that, given his occupation.

"But we don't meet anywhere. What, do I have to give up who I am to have a marriage? Do I have to become a stranger in my own house?"

"Maybe. Maybe it's just a matter of patience. You know in the spiritual life, it's always a matter of dying. I must die to myself, to what I want. It's the only way. It brings life though. It's the only thing that does."

"You think things will change if I wait it out?"

"They might. But you've got to pray. Pray always."

"Prayer, huh. I don't know. What does it get you?" And he told the priest about the life flights, the healers, about all the happy faces.

"Well, 'man makes his plans, God directs his feet,'" the priest said, offering the little girl his bag of peanuts. "Who knows what will happen. The Fat Lady hasn't sung yet, has she? Hold on."

She tossed it over to her Dad. "Think fast, Daddy," she said, delighted at her own joke. She jumped up on his lap, settled quickly in, ripping the bag open.

"I finds it's easy to forget what counts in all this speed and distraction, don't you? It's hard to even remember that there IS a lasting peace, let alone keep it. The modern world fragments people; it drives everyone apart. . . . It makes me shudder sometimes when I think about how it all might end."

Keith looked around at the thinly-peopled cabin, every one at least two seats apart from the closest person. "Yes, I guess it has."

He felt better as he got off the plane with a rosary in his hand. When he got back home, Ruthie raced in ahead of him. He dropped his keys on the expensive coffee table and looked at Katie who was staring back at him dumbfounded, and apologized for his immaturity.

At first Katie didn't answer. She dropped to one grateful knee and looked at Ruthie solemnly, or rather, looked over Ruthie, as if she were checking for parts, bruises. Was she okay? And then, as if that blow weren't enough, it came, the painfully excessive and showy hugging and kissing of her daughter's face, the too grateful tears, the accompanying moans. And what COULD he do but stand there and watch, a prisoner, being flogged before his execution?

The painful magnanimity of it all continued. She sat her husband down, held both of his hands and announced, grandly he felt, that she had decided last night to forgive him were he to come back, and that she would not break that promise she had made to herself. She said she knew he had not been himself of late, and that he was under a lot of stress. She and his mother, the whole church had been praying for his deliverance. (His mom in fact was still prostrated there in the upper room.)

What could he say? He WAS guilty. But he wondered, too, if he could ever really live here again. It now seemed to him as if he had given up all say in his life, that she had all the cards. If he wanted out, the payment due would be his daughter, his son; that and half the estate, which he had built, and through his sweat had maintained.

Katie, though, genuinely loved him, and with perhaps the best of intentions held him that night and rocked him in bed, his head to her breast, singing hymns. He didn't want any of it. Still, grotesquely, he let her do it. What choice did he have? He decided to live as quietly as he could within the silent walls of this place and wait.

Besides, he knew deep down that underneath his stunned and inert sensibility, he loved her, too, in his way, despite this madness. His two babies as well. God, if He were up there, on another plane, could surely take care of this. He would have to.

He prayed his beads three times a day and asked for the grace to forgive her real and imagined slights. He read the

Catholic spiritual books the priest had suggested him: STORY OF A SOUL; TRUE DEVOTION TO MARY; LOST IN THE WORLD, FOUND IN CHRIST. He was amazed at the kind of religion these beads offered. And he liked the priest he met, but didn't know if he wanted to become a Catholic. Still, the prayers brought him a lot of peace, and he appreciated that. And to his surprise, the joy of the game seemed slowly to seep back into the enterprise, the complete living in the present that comes with the full tilt chasing of a pop fly, flipping the ball to a fan. He reveled again in the feel of good wood and the dust that came with an agile slide or metaphorically with a practical joke.

He was beginning to feel alive again. And in an effort to keep this, his peace, in order to try and keep the applecart on all its wheels—the team was going great— he eventually stopped talking to reporters, all of whom seemed suddenly uncharitable in their pursuits for stories. He wanted just to play again, in the real sense of that word.

Tyrone, once he noticed the snub, congratulated him on his perspicacity. "Avoid the contentious SOBs, I say."

It was in late May when the reporter, John Maxwell, first saw him out there. Beto had taken to coming in an hour or so earlier than anyone, just to walk around the park, pray, clear his head. He still couldn't quite catch onto where Katie was coming from, much as he tried. He even gave his life to Jesus in one of her services, though he never did get the gift of tongues or experience anything tangible. No bells or whistles. Still, he felt he loved her, even admired her to a degree for her faith and courage, in the face of him mostly.

His mother was still a pain of course, shoveling him literature about the Baptism of the Holy Ghost, about healing services. She prayed with him hard, repeatedly, unsuccessfully; that he might get tongues. But it never happened.

And then she and Katie, still a team, prayed hard that their faith would be great enough to affect a healing in Tommy. They continued to take him to different states, countries, all the time denying that theirs was "a religion of works," a phrase he'd read about, one they used when discussing his newly discovered interest in Catholicism.

"Some God heals, some he doesn't," they'd say, and then they'd be right back at it, in their best "perseverance of the saints": fine clothes and permed hair, loud and long prayers, evidence, it seemed to him, of their elected status. The whole routine had gotten so common that he just blankly registered each failure when the "earned" healing did not happen.

Something, to their minds, had to be interfering. They kept claiming the healing; they threw out fleeces before the Lord, solicited prayer from renowned TV ministers: all the prayer requests piled before them as if they were the saints in heaven.

It was a nice break for him, to get to home games hours early, to feel the good breezes, the sunshine warm his hair, his shoulders, just the sounds of his beads, making their little noises against his thigh. The distant traffic, the occasional horn didn't bother him as high buildings, like big brothers, rose up around him.

He felt so good, alive, as if there were clear water fountaining up inside him. And to show his appreciation, he knelt down right there in the middle of the field and raised his hands, gave audible thanks to God.

On the fourth such day a peace larger than his own seemed to draw him toward it. Still on his knees, he went into it gladly, heard a crackling like static electricity or thunder as he saw little bits of yellow light.

II.

And yet again this century, that most glorious fissure of time and space happens in the middle of the air as the mystical rose opens. The layers of substance: blue sky, steel, which separate men from the indefinable glories of heaven begin, in a audible crinkle, to unpeel, give way, to curl back in a rippling of God light. The Most High Creator of the universe again breaks through and onto the tangible plane, bringing His peace, His most pure physicality, this time, as so often before, in the midst of His Mother's hidden smile.

She comes she says because God, her Son, wants to glorify her, because He has asked her to. He asks her again, as before, to reveal the structure of what is timeless for time. He asks her to reveal something of the plan, the stretch of what will be in words that have already been spoken, and yet for men, are still to be. Because all of time, for God, the Crucified One, is eternally present.

She comes to tell them what to do, because they are slow and need the repetition. Pray, fast, repent. "Do what He tells you." Live the Gospel.

And Keith, awed at the initial crackling sound, at the yellow glow he saw flicker in front of him, wondered what was happening? He was awed by the silence, by the sense of expectation he felt, not only in himself, but in the very grass as well as it seemed to stiffen, settle, away from the breezes. He felt it in the quiet air, as if the physical world itself were leaning in, listening, as if the rocks were getting ready to shout. He was anxious, heard a voice.

"Do not be afraid."

The Queen of Heaven appeared, soft, beautiful, in her smile, and what could the young person do but forget his own reservations, smile back. She was clad in the white of Fatima, though he wouldn't have known that, and thanked him for having said the prayers.

She asked him to pray even more fervently, to meditate on those mysteries of Incarnation, Redemption, Heaven, for lost souls especially. "And fast, Keith, when you can. From food, yes, but especially from sin. God is very much displeased with the world."

He didn't quite understand the scope of the message. "I know. I shouldn't have gone to Florida."

"Yes, your life is where to begin. Katie does love you."

"I don't understand her."

"Yes, but how much is for you to understand? Do not hold forth on what is beyond you. That's not what you're called to. . . . Love her, love and protect her. Be little. Pray to St. Joseph. . . . Jesus will be pleased. . . . And do not worry. The evil of the day is sufficient thereof. . . . Persevere." And then she talked about sin, told him what it was and suggested instruction. Before she left that first time, she told him she would see him again tomorrow.

Keith went three for four that day, smiling around the bases. He came home with a bouquet of flowers in one hand, a big statue of Mary tucked under the other. Katie beamed, she was pleased to see that her prayers were having an effect. She loved the flowers and put them in a vase, but didn't understand the statue.

"I know you're new to the Christian life, Keith. But that's idolatry," she said, tousling his hair. "Let's put that away." And she placed it outside the door.

Ruthie and Tommy, who was finally home, both liked the flowers as Katie lifted them up, one by one to have a smell. Keith delighted in their pleased faces. Tommy's bags—beneath his eyes—were, as always, packed, but he had such ready, bright twinkle, a smile as clean as any Keith had ever seen. Without guile, his whole soul participating in his every action. He'd arch his back as he lay there looking up at his Dad, kicking all four of his wonderful limbs up at him.

That night his wife seemed to go out of her way to make him comfortable: she got him an extra pillow for in front of the TV and put on a Sesame Street video, popped some corn. She massaged his shoulders as they watched and began to talk about her day.

When he woke up the next morning, the flowers were in a vase on the table in the breakfast room and the statue in the garbage outside.

Wells was a simple man. He liked this woman who kept appearing to him. She was nice, had a beautiful, welcoming smile. It made him feel good. He could learn from her.

Sometimes, early on, she came in different ways: one time she stood on a globe with a serpent beneath her heel. It writhed with its tail slapping the sphere, trying in the throws of death to wrap her leg. Another time she came with twelve stars around her head. During a third apparition she held the Infant, His heart pierced, emitting streams of water and blood.

She called herself "The Healing Mother," and told him that God cries out for His broken children. "Tell them to come. Tell them all to come. I want Jesus to be glorified. After mercy comes justice. Hell is real. There would be no freedom without it. Tell them that. Tell them, please, to come."

Keith was surprised by her emotion at first, as he was by the stream that immediately appeared in the outfield.

Okay. He would tell them he finally decided, but how?

Peoples was the first one taken by the change in him. It was only three weeks since his AWOL episode, and yet he seemed more together than anybody else on the team. He clowned around less and expressed a more hearty, if quiet good fellowship: the slap on the shoulder that stayed there for a minute.

Wells worked as hard as ever, as least as far as Tyrone could see, but he seemed now to enjoy the work on a deeper level. You could see that in his eyes and his manner. He stopped breaking things: light bulbs, water coolers when the hits didn't come. He seemed to seek out those players he liked least. Was it his latest version of "team," or had something more profound happened to him? Tyrone suspected the latter as there seemed a peace in the guy; you could palpably feel it when you stood next to him. And so he decided, approached him one day as both were walking out of the tunnel to the parking lot.

"Hey, man. What's up?"

"Our pitching. Can you believe those guys?" They both laughed, but Peoples would not be put off.

"Na, na. That ain't what I mean. . . . What's come over you? You've changed, gotten more grease or something."

"Oh that." Keith smiled. "Prayer mostly, I guess."

"Well take me to that church. I want to drink some of that water."

That jolted Wells. "Well, it IS a pretty weird story."

"I got no problems with weird. Come over with it."

And though the two of them had never been very close, Wells told him everything. That he had discovered real prayer, or rather, that it had been revealed to him. Infused contemplation the books said. It was often like your whole being walked in sunlight: the green cross-cut grass, the blue sky, fountains and fountains of living water that leaped up into summer air. Even the car noises outside brought him joy. He now found himself amazed as he got his ankles taped: the movement of the joints, the precision of the trainer. All of it gave God glory. Couldn't he see that? And even if we blow it, we can repent and come back. God is able.

Tyrone thought the man was getting off.

"I am, T. On Jesus and on the Holy Spirit. With the help of his Mother."

"His Mother? Now that's new to me. I used to go to my Momma's church in Shreveport when I was a kid, and people'd be dropping like croppers in the heat, singing that good old religion until they fell somewhere else. Nice for awhile. But it never lasted much past show time. Then it was chicken on the front porch when we got back home."

"Well, I'm pretty new to all of this, but I don't think you can try to keep it. It's all a gift. You've just got to be open to it and let it change the ordinary world."

"Yeah, okay, maybe. But what about this Mother thing? Are you becoming Catholic or something?"

"No, it's becoming me." And Keith told him all about his first vision of the Lady. He'd never even thought about joining the Church, so he knew it wasn't all in his head. T. could come with him tomorrow if he wanted to. But don't tell anybody, at least not yet.

Tyrone couldn't sleep much that night, reasoned to himself that he didn't have anything against religion or prayer. It was just that it had never done much for him. Life led him in other directions. Of course none of them were especially satisfying either, but the house he lived in sure beat the limits that he felt had been put on him back in Louisiana.

He missed his parish though. His mother, his uncle, Mardi Gras costume battles, men like peacocks, each allowing his plumes and his strut to do his talking for him. It was a beat up world, but it was his. Or his Mother's to be more accurate. He could play there, eat her good food, and run free under her hand. She had provided love and protection whatever the trials. His own porch in the present was finer, but it seemed somehow white too. Maybe that had to do with the notion of "success," materialism, owning things. Not to show them off, but to have them with the pretense that you were NOT sporting your own feathers.

He didn't know in the end, but he would take it. It beat the hell out of an empty belly or the borders of beat up neighborhoods. If you had a fine enough car and dressed conservatively enough, there were few places you could not go. And with that he finally fell asleep.

When he got to the stadium, he saw Wells walking around in the outfield in his bare feet. Nature boy. Well the guy was at least goofy enough to do that. He yelled across the field. When he saw the big smile, Tyrone addressed him.

"So where's the Lady?"

"She said she'll be here. Come on." And Tyrone followed, feeling acutely foolish. What was he doing this for? He looked around quickly to make sure no one was watching. When they knelt down he tried to keep his eyes to himself, remember a hymn, but he couldn't help occasionally looking over at Wells as the latter went over his beads and said his strange prayers. There was a dim smile on his face until the Lady came.

At that point his face jerked so quickly upward that it made Tyrone flinch. He didn't see anything himself, but did hear a humming sound. Watching with amazement, he tried to make out what Wells was saying, couldn't. So he got up and walked around, to behind where the Lady seemed to be appearing. He wanted to look at Well's face, into his eyes. The man was definitely seeing something.

To further convince himself of that fact, he moved his hand in front of his teammate's eyes to prevent Wells from seeing. He held it there for a second. Then he pulled it away quickly. It didn't matter. Wells had the same blissful look on his face, the same moving lips.

And finally after summoning up the courage, he tried to move the second baseman, push him off his pins. No luck. The guy was rooted in the spot like stone. In the end he settled for a spot on the pitcher's mound. He'd just have to wait.

That wasn't long in coming. Tyrone could see Wells relax and slowly come out of his trance. When he got up it was as if he'd forgotten that Tyrone was with him. In fact it wasn't until Wells started walking off the field, until Tyrone bumped him, that Wells even remembered he had company.

"Man, what did you see?"

"You didn't see her?"

"No. But I know you do. What is all this about anyway?"

"She says Jesus wants to heal people here, that we should tell them and invite them to come."

"Are you crazy? Yeah, tell them. That'll go over big. Do you want to start a war? Do you think the powers that be are just going to let you take over a baseball season, their stadium, to conduct religious services to some lady only you see? You must be tripping."

"That's what she said."

Tyrone was concerned; he was starting to like this simple fellow, but what he was asking for was crazy. "Look, why don't you pray some more about it. I'll come with you. If she still says you should announce this at the beginning of the next homestand, I'll stand with you when you hold the press conference, okay?"

"Okay. I mean I'll ask her about it."

"So what else did she say?"

Tyrone's consternation must have been apparent, because by the next day there were three other players with them. They didn't see or hear much either, a crackling sound, something like glitter in the air, but all three were sufficiently moved to agree with Tyrone. Something was going on out there of a supernatural nature.

Word spread quickly throughout the clubhouse. The skies were opening behind second base. And when a few of the guys asked Wells about it, he told them as honestly as he could. Some lady was showing up, the Mother of God perhaps. "She's nice, has asked others to come. So you're welcome."

Members of the team's Bible group were disturbed and called a meeting. They were to a man very concerned. Some had heard of these types of things, but opinions were mixed. In most cases, many thought, it was Satan who appeared disguised as an angel of light; but others argued that many people started reading their Bibles more often in those places too. Surely that couldn't be evil. They were at a loss for what to do. Each wanted God to be glorified in all things, but what if this occurrence did have another place of origin?

So how should they handle it. Wally Westlake, the leader, suggested that they pray long and hard together here first and then that each go home after the game and diligently seek the Lord. They could all meet at his house at ten in the morning with the word each had gotten.

Each came back with some variation of the same message. "He is mine." "Love him." So what did that mean? Was

Jesus working on him through false apparitions, or were the apparitions true? They decided finally as a group that they should support their teammate whatever their personal beliefs. They all believed in prayer. And maybe by doing so, who knows, perhaps they could turn the focus of things to Jesus. Besides, news was bound to leak, and they didn't need division during a pennant chase. They would support him in principle. If there was one thing the world definitely needed it was prayer.

As a group they decided that they would go to today's apparition just to check things out. After that each player was on his own. Each could go or not go, whatever his preference. They would, however, it was emphasized, continue verbal support of Wells, prayer, whatever their decisions. They would ignore the whole thing during games and after.

Unknown to all of them, of course, there was an eye in the mezzanines: Maxwell. He saw all ten of them and felt that he had to break the story.

Each of them saw the morning paper and knew what effect the story would have. And each one of them, without consulting the others, was moved to show up for a second consecutive day. They, too, had felt the peace. Besides, they had to support their teammate for what was sure to be an uncomfortable day.

They were not disappointed. 600 fans showed up. Most were respectful, but some jeered as well. They wanted hits, not prayers. Pray for a pennant.

Westlake didn't like being there, praying before onlookers, being mocked as he did so. His feelings were mixed. He felt like an early Christian in the Coliseum, but he felt some anger at Wells, too, for bringing all this on. He opened his Bible while kneeling to get some consolation and read the words of the 23rd Psalm. He was surprised to find that the words came alive for him as they never had before. Something WAS going on here, but he fought the impulse to embrace it. It was too alien, potentially dangerous.

After it was over he talked to the press about the incident. Yes, they supported Wells. No, they didn't think he was crazy. Everybody should pray more, especially those in the press.

He felt for Wells, who looked a little disoriented. He really had no idea what he'd done here. What would become of him, Westlake wondered? Reporters laughed as he passed, made comments as he took his turn, late, in the batting cage. And it would only get worse. So Westlake exhorted his teammate above the clamor, drowned them out, was joined by a few of the other guys.

As for himself, Wells was surprised. Why should everyone get on him for something he had absolutely nothing to do with? And she was such a nice person. If they had any sense, they'd come themselves. Well, they obviously didn't. So he wasn't going to worry about them, or anybody. They chose the world they lived in.

His resolve was soon tested as the whole pagan nation descended the following week. He refused to talk to anybody, just took what the other players dished out at the beginning. That actually helped him, made him center himself even more at the plate. As more and more hits came, opponents said less and less on the field. (A few first basemen would even join him in a Hail Mary as he took his lead off first.)

And although his teammates never said much about it to him, many of them found the national media sideshow a blessing in ways they hadn't expected. Whatever they did or failed to do became second page material. They could run around the bases backwards with their pants down and not have gotten noticed. Without the pressure, they could go about their jobs and keep winning games. They could slide in and out of town, take a quick 2 of 3 or 4 of 4, move off the vaudevillian stage with high stealthy steps, their shoes in their hands as Wells, a latter day St. Sebastian, took the arrows.

At home, arrows were delivered at a much closer range. Katie, when she found out about it, gave him the silent treatment for a long time. The only noises he heard where the ones she made when she was cleaning, all much louder than usual. She had long shared a tacit, ingrained suspicion of the Catholic Church with many of her fellow church members. How could he do this to her?

But as news people kept calling at all hours, she found

she couldn't contain her anger any longer. They wanted her reaction. Did she hear the story about the woman with the eye? It grew right back into her head. Did "Our Lady of the Outfield" appear to her as well, and if she really had healed people why hadn't her husband gotten her to heal their son? Were they at odds? A neighbor had mentioned marital problems. Why did her husband go down so early to the park anyway? The people had a right to know.

She had to chase reporters away from her front door with a broom and endure them as they'd park right out in front of her house, stop any neighborhood kid or adult who happened to be passing by. They went through her garbage, sneaking around at all hours, knocking over the cans, looking in windows. They shouted across the lawn when she came out for her mail and insisted again that the story belonged to the people. It was undemocratic, unchristian, and un-American for her to keep the truth from them.

At last she conceded and offered to talk to one reporter, Jane Smalley. Katie told her that she was a Christian and didn't care about religions of works. Yes, they had had problems, but who hasn't? No, she hadn't spoken much to him about it at all. It was a sore subject; she was an Evangelical Pentecostal Christian after all. She said what really bothered her was that she could no longer attend games because of this. The people were just too rude. She told the reporter that she'd finally just cut herself off from that part of their lives, didn't care about what went on at the ball park. She cared about her family and her privacy.

But the interview didn't help. In fact it only fanned the flames. THE NATIONAL ENQUIRER followed her around the supermarket and hounded her with obnoxious questions as she searched for cereal. Had her husband ever undergone any psychological treatment? What about aliens or Elvis, had he seen them as had been reported?

Photographers were especially inventive. She spotted more than one in the trees across the street with telephoto lens. They found their way into her church services, into a neighbor's pool party where her friends quickly chased them off. Finally, she just steeled herself and decided that she would not let these people get to her. And she did well, look-

by them. Next week it would be someone else. All she had to do was ride in out for the duration.

Inside curtained windows, however, a different drama was unfolding. Katie raged at her husband and accused him of doing all this to get back at her. He had lied, she said, crying, claimed to become a Christian only to hurt her. The altar calls were false, weren't they? If he hated her that much why did he marry her? How could he do this to her? How could he go pope-ing, how could he expect her to let a worshipper in the synagogue of Satan have spiritual headship over her? Or was he just that stupid? Did he know what people called the Catholic Church? The whore of Babylon! It's in the Book of Revelation for Pete's sake. Didn't he have a clue in the world?

And how did he expect her to face the congregation? And what about the children? Did he expect her to raise them in a split home, baptize any other children they might have as Catholics? Well he could forget that. And did he know that this was a reason enough for divorce?

He tried to stay steady, let it pass.

Which was more than she was willing to do. She kept trying: different intensities, different approaches. What about his career? What about the life they had built together? Did he think management was going to take this lying down now that it was in the news, and them right in the middle of a pennant race? No one was that important to the team. And how would he be able to continue playing after the whole charade was over? Did he ever think of that? He would be a laughing stock as long as he set foot on any field.

She finally left and took the children over a friend's house. She would not let him destroy her children's lives, all for the sake of his ego, because he HAD to win in this little war they were having, because he had to give it a religious face. It seemed so diabolical to her the more she thought of it. He was using false religion to protest the rightful place of true religion in her life. It had made him uncomfortable. Well, isn't that too bad?

He called her every day, though, told her he loved her, needed her. Sometimes he told her about the Virgin, what she looked like that day, what she had to say. He would "Love, love, love, and never count the cost" because that's what the Gospel asked. And if at first she didn't want to hear that, the time away from her good home made her miss it. She began to remember the good times.

They eventually began to talk for long periods. On some days she'd even laugh. But on others the hurdles seemed too high for her, and his exasperating perpetual "humility" only made matters worse.

She couldn't take that and told him so. He was a joke. How could he do this: make false piety the battlefield where they fought for the fate of their children? He was twisted and made her so angry, setting himself up on a charger as the virtuous one. What was she, wrong because she wanted to please God? Wrong because she valued heaven more than earth?

After she slammed the phone down one day she felt remorse. She was not being Christian. But how could Jesus do this to her? Everything had been going so well. She only wanted to be faithful. Finally it occurred to her that meant loving Keith too, whatever their future relationship. What reward could she expect, after all, loving only Christians?

And love, as it always does, opened doors. She moved back in, their conversations became more civil. He asked her why she disliked Catholics so much anyway? He didn't know much about it, but weren't all denominations brothers and sisters in Christ? Besides it wasn't like he chose to have Mary appear to him. That was her idea. Had he ever mentioned her before this thing? Had he ever mentioned Catholicism at all? What did Katie want him to do, tell her to go back to heaven?

No, he didn't think she was a devil in disguise. Everything she had said up until that point had been very scriptural: fast, pray, return to her Son. What was wrong with that? And why shouldn't Jesus love His mother too, want her loved? They both loved their mothers. Surely that was not a surprising attitude. Would they mind if someone saw the virtue in their mothers? And besides, what solely human person could possibly know more about the Holy Spirit than Mary anyway? Did she ever think how odd that sounds, Pentecostals, of all people, disclaiming her?

And then he expressed his loneliness. Did she think this was easy, some joy ride for him? The press, the fans treated him with contempt; other players felt too nervous around him to talk, to him or to each other; his own wife wouldn't even look him in the eye. And where was he supposed to go to church now? A lot of the Catholics he'd met since this whole thing started told him to go back to the church he'd come from, that Mary was an impediment. What did he know about visions anyway? Why was he chosen? Maybe she could go sit in for him tomorrow.

And with that he sunk into his chair, looked straight ahead, at nothing in particular. It moved Katie. So she went over to where he sat and knelt down in front of him. She put a hand on his cheek and looked at him as she hadn't for a long while. "Hey. I'm here," she said.

He sighed, refocused, pressed the crown of his head next against hers for a long time. "Thank you."

But then he got nervous, rose, and began to pace before finally stopping in the middle of the room. "She said there was going to be many healings," he said, looking outside. "Things are going to get a lot weirder."

She bowed her head for a moment, still kneeling where she'd been and looked at the backs of her fingers. Then she got up, looked at him for a second, and turned and dipped under his arm which she'd raised.

"If this is of God, there's no need to worry. . . . All he wants is our lives."

But she did worry on nights when she couldn't sleep; she'd see him right next to her, working those beads between his fingers.

To escape the media posse, Keith began to move Katie and the children from best hotel to best hotel, in whichever town the team happened to be in. They'd wear sunglasses, he a mustache to take in the museums, the amusement parks. Ruthie loved it.

At home, with the help of the team, he rented a warehouse downtown. The kids had lots of floor space to play on and windows to look out of, and the yuppies didn't mind, took to the children in fact. Especially Tommy. They'd bring both children little gifts and toys: baby briefcases, doctor's stethoscopes, would wax protective when any suspicious news-like person came near.

Katie was much more at home with their relationship now, and Keith was glad of that. It was she in fact who suggested they go back to their house one night and put a dummy in the window with its head in its hands. Both thoroughly enjoyed the letter they got from Julia and Gerry: a PEOPLE magazine picture of Katie, stiffly at a kitchen table, apparently catatonic in despair.

He ordered flowers for her each day and took her dancing to restaurants he'd have to rent for the evening. Just the two of them, and a band sometimes, the extra waiters/waitresses playing cards at another table.

But as much as she loved him, stood by him, she was not convinced about Mary. She was an Evangelical, after all; she didn't need any other intercessor. If it was good and Biblical, then it was fine for him. Just don't expect her to change.

Still, she was generous in her response and gave him the space, the ride he needed as he took his RCIA classes. She'd give him an occasional question to ask, hoping to find flaws in his Catholic, as she called it, armor.

Was he worshipping Mary yet?

Well, he did honor her, as Christ did his mother. He told her that the Hebrew word for honor, "kaboda," means "to glorify."

How can you find Biblical support for the Pope?

He took out books, asked questions of his tutors, who asked questions of theirs. Well, first there was the name: "Peter," and then, of course, the pledge, but he also found out some curious information about the "keys" reference. When Jesus spoke of the "keys of the kingdom," he was, it appeared, speaking in the understood, handed-down context of the Old Testament. When Hezekiah replaced David's Prime

Minister, Shebna with Eliakim, he gave him the "keys to the kingdom." Interesting, don't you think? The "keys" are intended to symbolize Peter's primacy as Prime Minister, literally the "first minister," the Pope.

They hacked away for hours, debated what exactly the idea of covenant meant, just what was meant by justification, was sola scriptura found anywhere in scripture? They talked about the Councils of Hippo and Carthage, each consulting his or her experts, each armed with his and her books. And though he came up with complete answers for her every concern, still there was something deeply ingrained in her that resisted. Her country, her reformed religion were after all in large part built on, he would say, an over-zealous appreciation of the intellect, its place. Submission to this degree was an alien concept, something foreign to the American character, at least when it came to anything that was not American. (No one of course would doubt the importance of submission in the military, especially when it came time for war.)

They both enjoyed the vigor of their exercises, and it brought them closer together though there was little given on either side. Still, Katie began to feel some respect, appreciation for her husband, for what he was doing and going through. But she felt pangs of jealousy also. How was she supposed to compete with a heavenly woman, if she were appearing? She was by all accounts kind, wise, compassionate, the mother of Christ, not the shrew Katie knew she had too often been with her husband.

But she knew, too, that hers was not to reason why and so she plowed on in serving his meals and in loving him as best she could, trying to die to herself daily.

As far as the baseball end of things went, he was enjoying this season as he hadn't others for some time. Sure there was madness: the push of the crowd, the constant hoots, the apples, silent teammates. But it was still a child's game, this thing in front of him, and he had early on decided to treat it like one, run with the joy of running, hit because it felt good. He couldn't really decide if he liked hitting or base running better. The importance of hitting was obvious and he loved doing that, but on the base paths, now there you could cause some real panic, take the heart out of your opponent.

Mary liked baseball, told him jokingly that she had the best seat in the house. But it was the world, too, she said, with its greed and materialism. And that was everywhere. He must pray, pray. That was the only thing holding God back. She said further that while a few had been healed up until that time, that God had permitted that many more should be so. He was going to do something here the likes of which He had never done before.

It was only a week before the White Sox were to come in for a crucial game that she had him announce that she would cure all those suffering from M.D. and M.S. on July 2nd at 10:00.

It was an off day, at least for the players. Buses and specially-rigged vans started showing up at six in the morning. Groundskeepers tried not to watch as more than 1300 wheel chairs rutted their way through grass and infield dirt. There was an air of expectation pervading the field, and as they waited, many of the afflicted as well as those accompanying them prayed together while waiting for Wells.

He worked his way through the crowd because she had asked him to, part of him repulsed by this sea of gnarled bodies, voices clamoring at him, voices he could not understand. And the limbs, all those crooked arms, reaching for him as if he could give them what they needed. Was it so much to understand he wanted to ask? This didn't come from him. This stuff came from somewhere else.

But he thought, too, of the others. So many people were starving all over the world and so many innocent ones were being slaughtered while a few heedless gluttons divvied up the land and the cars and the food. The end of the world would have to be so spectacular when it came he decided; there would have to be an accompanying joy SO spontaneous, SO pervasive that the very face of the earth would be changed. Otherwise how could everyone forget centuries of this. Maybe joy and forgiveness would come and come in waves, rippling out from the center, with everyone getting off the hook, all because of what the Lamb in the middle had done.

That was not Scriptural, he knew, so he did not hang his hat on it. But it did sound a lot like God.

At first it was only one of them here and one of them there. People beginning to feel all of their limbs for the first time, beginning to feel them straighten. For the first time they felt ease in movement. Then others. And before long, amid a great sound of moans chairs were being knocked over as new people got up, some of them quickly, each of them beginning to praise God and to shout in jubilation.

Within fifteen minutes they were all standing, wet with tears, many in the arms of their attendants. What had God done! At one time, marveled Keith. Surely now people would believe. 1,328, it was later confirmed, were made whole on that one day.

Presses all over the world covered it. The prediction had come true. Surely this must be the Mother of God appearing. And it stayed in all the papers, for four days. But then, slowly, the jokes started appearing: suggestions about lotto tickets, the Belmont Stakes, and after that, monumental cries for global justice, rage over pestilence, wars, and eventually, the kind of resentment that comes like the closing of a huge iron door.

Katie was flabbergasted. Should she become Catholic, join the religion she had for so long detested? What was going on out on that field? Maybe she SHOULD bring Tommy. She hoped though that Keith didn't expect her to go running around sharing her testimony if she did convert.

The All-Star game was a big success. The whole stadium took a moment of silence to ask for God's blessing on all those in need; the Bishop even threw out the first ball. But people have short attention spans, so when the newspapers had a heavenly field day with the home players' success in that game, using every religious metaphor in existence to make their slightly comic points, well, it wasn't long before the common religious impulse began to fade. Many people began to complain; they wanted to forget about God during the week. They wanted to watch a ballgame.

Maybe their reaction was to be expected in some way; maybe these people were put off by the vandals, or by all that would have been expected of them were they to fully embrace this divine occurrence. Whatever the reason for the waning of interest on their part though, the surrounding circus continued full force.

Every anti-Christian group had its day on the news, in court. The Madelaine Murray O'Hare and Hemlock Societies protested vigorously. And even though the healings kept occurring at a phenomenal rate, so did the violent behavior of those who sought disorder. Many people banded together, asked that she leave. It was all too much. Things were boring before, but they were peaceful. We didn't have to deal with mobs or miracles.

Keith was concerned, and when he asked the Lady why there had to be all this violence, she told him not to worry, that Satan was going through his death rattle. His time was short and he knew it. He would snap at her heels and cause her all the difficulty he could until the time came for her to crush his head. It was all the pathetic creature had. But she told Keith again that he shouldn't worry. God, who still hangs on the cross, and who will until the end of time, turns all things to good for those that love Him.

Tyrone was stunned by the mass healings. He had been coming almost daily until they started happening. Then he decided to stay away. This was too big, too much for him. How could he keep coming unless he really believed? God would strike him dead.

But Keith reassured him. Come! Come! The impulse to come was reason enough. God would do the rest. So, reluctantly, he did. But it all scared him. Where would all this end? He was no believer, not a member of this club, though he was somewhat re-assured when he saw a large Nigerian contingent, beating their drums, dancing in their brightly colored dashikis.

It distressed him that he had always been on the outside, for his whole life. That's where he got his power from, that's what gave him his fight. (He was leading the league in home runs, RBI's.) And part of him liked it that way. Would he have to give it all up to be part of this? Yes, he knew. He would. But he couldn't quit coming now. He wasn't sure of anything except that he had two feet to bring him. He HAD to see what would become of this.

By the time the Yankees showed up in September, Wells was beginning to feel the wear of an imposed responsibility, the wear of a pennant race. Vandalism was reaching epidemic proportions, as were the healings. But more and more people seemed to be responding negatively to the whole thing. Many demanded that he be traded, that he take this whole show elsewhere. They were just a city of pretty good neighborhoods. They didn't need this madness. They had children and a way of life to protect. Who cared if he was hitting .340, who cared if they were in first place even? There were more important things. They wanted their old lives back.

What saved him was that a lot of people didn't want their old lives back. They wanted to change as people; they wanted a pennant. And if they had to go through a little madness to get those things, then so be it. Because, unlike the former folk, they remembered their little neighborhoods back before all this started. All the little irritants. And what was there to talk about? What was there to make them feel good?

Games had to be played later at night because of the crowds and the healings. And that wasn't the only thing that changed. The Indians, unable to stem the tide of pilgrims, decided to become one as an organization. They gathered together every winged and dinged player in their system and funneled them to the services. And in that three week span, they, like most everyone else who came, were healed. Anterior cruciate ligaments, rotator cuffs, deep thigh bruises. So what could the owners do? They kind of enjoyed it after awhile. (They had insurance, after all.) They did what they could to get the games in, acknowledging to the press that deference was important here. Something greater than baseball was happening at this field.

And to help expedite matters they got Keith seven secretaries to keep up with the mails. People asked if he would touch an enclosed handkerchief? They could put it over their little girl's eye or throat or spine. They asked him if they should they buy this house? Accept this job? Would he come to their high school reunion or speak to a youth group?

His own wife brought Tommy repeatedly late in September. But though his ear canals widened, his muscle tone become more pronounced, and his joints tightened, he did not lose his disability. Katie wept and wanted to know why not? Didn't he have as much right and dignity as other people? Couldn't he serve God better if he were made whole? Mary, in reply, asked her though Keith if anything but good had come out of his condition.

And even Katie, angered though she still was, had to admit that was so. She herself had often noticed the way people responded to him. Inevitably they lit up. Even Katie's parents had come around. They didn't take it so personally now, had even begun to talk to Keith as if he were a human being.

The whole thing, he thought, was a spectacle right out of Cecil B. DeMille. And he asked her: why had she chosen him? He was a sinful man. Because she loved him, she said, because he would listen.

But that was no answer. God did what He did because He did it. "Trust the omniscient One" was Keith's favorite joke. HE was the only one who could do that handshake. But Keith knew too at a deeper level that this would be his last year. How could there be any more seasons after this? He'd already punched some guy who'd come out onto the field after him. What would he do next year or the year after when she wasn't around? He couldn't ask his teammates to continue to be the buffer between him and the world.

Only Peoples stuck with him through the whole ordeal. Because Tyrone liked him, Keith knew that, because he got only good things from the apparitions. But Keith suspected there were others reasons as well, Ty's own.

And he was right. Tyrone had scores to settle. And this was a good way to strike his own blows as well. He had never had much affection for the world and its workings, and this was a way to widen his circle of contempt past the press and everything they stood for. Here he could expand it to include the whole world with its ingrained falseness whatever the latest mask of justice.

As a boy, how many times had he seen it, felt it. Humiliation due to a coincidental, due to something no one had any control over. The pigment of one's skin. It was all ugly and absurd. And he resented the hell out of it, the stupidity of the world, the shallowness, the extent of people's fears. He couldn't understand. If they were THAT afraid, why not go down into themselves and see what was at the heart of all that? Why choose to remain on such a shallow and superstitious level.

White people amazed him; they were all literally terrified of their shadows. To them he was their dark side, the collective workings of the primal unconsciousness: death, chaos. The boogie man.

He had his own fears of course. He knew that. But he wasn't going to let them slow him down. His whole life was the tool he would use to beat that superstitious stupidity on the level it was enforced. He would succeed on their terms, make enough money to almost appear as one of them. He, like others before him, would be the silent stick in their craw. He would be a friendly boogie man, and every white person knows how scary that can be.

And now this. The lady coming, asking him too to go down and see the root of who he was and what he needed. Yes. He knew. Underneath his rage and all the saving effort it summoned, he was a man who needed to be shown the right way as much as anyone else. And a large, deeper part of him wanted that Way too. But the rest of him resisted, knew too what was at risk. His success, life as he knew it.

He had been using that anger for so long, letting it eat at his liver like a live bird each time he came up to bat that he didn't know what would become of him if he tried to let it go. And though deep down he knew his rage probably would shorten his life, still it gave him a decisive edge as well. So he came, waited. Let her change him if she wanted. He'd come like the man he was: stuck, searching, and fierce.

And if he was wrong in his worldly assessments, he wasn't so by a large margin. All one had to do to see that this was a white man's game was look up into the owners' box. For them, as far as he was concerned, he was a highly valued piece of meat, an Apollo without any real Creed. And in a way, he knew he couldn't win there either. The higher his asking price, the more he acknowledged their higher station.

Then let them both prosper, he had finally decided. The owners could delight in having the finest commodity; he could steal the family silver.

And he DID like the game. In it he could be judged objectively, by the numbers he put up. But that very "objectivity" caused him problems as well, even as it offered solutions. Here, like always, the black man was rendered invisible. Who he was as a person did not matter. It was just another example of the nature of this world. Any up side had a down. Whatever the accomplishment: April 15, 1947 or "Brown vs. the Board of Education," there was always the down side of the pendulum. Could she change that he wondered?

He'd never found Wells terribly bright, but he WAS there for Tyrone when he broke into the big house. Never said a word about Burlington either. T. had appreciated that. So when the microscope came, Peoples figured it was time to settle things.

He knelt out there next to his teammate through the rest of that hot summer. Speaking volumes without ever opening his mouth. He just wanted to stand against. That was all of it really. And if he never learned any of these prayers, he did often find himself thinking about praying, moving his lips, praying the prayers his Mother had used back in Shreveport. In the First Baptist Church. All the purple robes swaying, tambourines and variation. Love in the face of overwhelming evidence to the contrary.

He liked the fact that now he was shaking his own larger, if invisible instrument at the world, at its smallness, its meanness, at its great and, he hoped, dying moan.

Even after Wells had gone, long after the season was over, Tyrone kept coming back and looking for what he had found there. He watched people pick through the rubble, watched old men and children strain as they teamed up and carried away heavy stones, dumping them into the sinking trunks of cars.

Strange as they were, they were a lot like him. They wanted answers as much as he did. And he watched the ridiculous effort they spent to get it. Did they think that a stone was going to help them? Did they need a relic to bring back a world that wasn't meant to last?

And he wondered, too, did the only world we really knew have to be ripped apart, turned upside down in order for folks to get what they really needed, whatever their mask. Without a doubt, he said, smiling to himself.

III.

To Keith and Katie's relief no calls came at the end of the season. There were no banquet invitations, no requests for interviews, no madness. It seemed as if people had forgotten him. "God hides whom He loves," as the French saying goes. And so it went with him.

He went back to the Field several times in disguise to pray not long after the apparitions had stopped. But this part of it was clearly over, despite the hundreds and hundreds of people who braved the opportunists and potentially dangerous conditions.

He looked around himself at the place. There were no bases left, no foul lines. What was left of the dugouts looked like would-be bomb shelters covered with graffiti, some kind of gang lettering. Large sections of seats and the foul poles were gone. The right center field fence bobbed, and he saw an apparently organized group of people high in the right field stands with what looked and sounded, late, like sledgehammers. Person to person, in a line, they passed each stone to the top of the wall, where the last person flipped it over the side. There was very little sod left, no bulbs left on the scoreboard.

The spring had come back again, pooled there in shallow center, pilgrims filling bottles and plastic milk containers. (She told him that would stay.) The whole thing made him sad. A large part of his life was over. All the friendships and all the camaraderie. Well, so be it.

Katie still didn't know about that part of it, the retirement, but she was grateful for his sake that the visions had stopped. Now at least they could be a family again. So she was happy when he put the house up for sale and sold it. She looked forward to taking off in their new Winnebago, just the four of them, without a radio or a TV or a newspaper, on a very slow trip out West.

Keith's parents were back together again, and everyone concerned looked forward to making that connection. It would be just folks with no worries, just an occasional walk under redwoods, maybe some fly fishing. But both of the younger couple looked forward to their meantimes as well.

They enjoyed what they could of graying and chilling Lake Erie water, just a few wisps of snow across Lake Road as they drove out of town. State highways offered the time they felt they needed and a view. They could check out the uniqueness of each little place, the local cuisine as they meandered their way across the country.

Since the weather was pretty cool the whole way back, they often chose to sit on top of the cruiser in lawn chairs and coats, hands wrapped around cups of warm cocoa in the evenings to catch the sun go home often until stars spoke of larger realities. Ruthie and Keith would duck under barbed wire fences in Kansas, grab some tumbleweed; they'd run with them across wide treeless fields. Katie would call them back eventually with a whistle, to games of Parcheesi or Candyland. (Tommy was still a little snippet, could offer little but a ready and unfettered smile, carrots in his hair.)

Katie had never seen the Rockies before, so they did a tour of Estes Park, later pulling the huge vehicle over on a dry gravel road on the western slope to read some Scripture, talk over what God had done.

When they got back home, the four adults got to spend some quality time together. No one talked about what had happened. They sat around and read or watched some movies in the evening. Eventually a few of his old friends even came over, every one mum on the holy subject. Games of volleyball were played out back; there were barbecues and dirt bikes. The couples took long walks when the weather allowed for it, went to state parks, the trees and then the blue ocean with, to Ruthie's delight, trawlers out on the water.

After a week of unwinding, Gerry suggested a fishing trip: just the two of them could go to his old cabin in British Columbia. They didn't talk much as they packed the boat and car and drove north through small Oregon and Washington towns, and they both liked it that way. When the times did come to punctuate the silences, Dad would talk nostalgically about the trips they'd taken in the past, razz the waitresses. Keith appreciated his Father's gesture, if not the results. He found himself still worrying what his next move would be? How would Katie take his retirement?

The old cabin was dusty and brought back memories: over-turned boats, the shallows, him walking the little creek alone when he was small. He remembered the sun-baked tops of the little stones, how they poked up like the heads of small playmates out of the tea-dark water. Maybe he could find that one spot again, where he could heave big rocks in the water, listen to them dunk and splash. Maybe he could find that high rock with a view. The cabin seemed like a part of his life he had too long neglected. It brought back the smell of frying fish and his friends' yells, the time he brought his first girl-friend up here.

But to both of their dismay it rained hard for the first two days. They made the best of it, left both windows open so they could catch the smells and sounds of water and the re-sponding green. Both delighted in the great wash of rain they heard. Or was it the ground water surging? Maybe both? They couldn't tell. But they did find comfort in this family place, in their silences and books, in the pipe smoke and sounds of testing reels. Like a couple of regular Noahs, it seemed to a smiling Keith. (He waited for the house to rock, eventually lift its way up off the ground.)

When they emerged on that third day, Keith found he wasn't far wrong. The constant downpour had soaked the ground so thoroughly that it no longer had a verifiable consis-tency to it. From an uneasy porch they could see the angry creek, close to the cabin to begin with, now surging, a full twelve feet wide just to their right. It seemed like some noisy reality to him reaching for the cabin footings. What was it, a new life?

Upstream, any trace of an identifiable creek bed was gone. There was a new configuration as the powerful light brown water humped like an angry animal, tossed and spit its almost-white fringe of spray, sweeping along everything in its path.

In their boat out on the high lake things were more peaceful. They had room now to finally talk. Keith's parents seemed more chummy these days than he could remember them ever being. But his Dad had never been big on religion, and if he had become a recent convert Keith knew he would have heard about it by now.

"What's up with you two, anyway? Are you and Ms. Express Yourself back together for good?"

"What. . . your Mother?? Oh. She is how she is, you know that. You can't change her."

"Yeah. That's her department."

"Well, it certainly wasn't all her fault, you know. . . . It never is."

"What's that mean?"

"Nothing much. Just that it takes two to make a marriage, two to make a problem."

"So what's the point?"

The older man laughed. "What I mean is that I only saw what I wanted to see. I was spending all my time pulling against instead of with. Mom made life comfortable, so I took it. I never gave anything. Or enough. It got to her, you know. She had to leave for awhile. . . . Look, no one knows any better than me how pushy, irrational, impulsive she can be, but I know too that she ain't alone on that ship."

And then Keith's Father threw him a curve. "Keith. . . you ever listen to jazz music?"

"Jazz. . . Dad, what, are you into that now? Are you blowing sax now or what?"

"No, but you've got to understand, son. . . . You're grown up and moved away now. Now we've got some space to fill, and not much time to fill it. . . . Mom's right there. I'm finding lots of new interests. . . . But back to my question."

"No, I don't know anything about jazz. . . . Rap, country. I've heard too much of that stuff."

"Well I ask because I want to make a point. On the piano, the right hand plays the melody for the most part, the left plays the base lines. . . .You even heard the expressions 'White Bread,' 'Vanilla.'"

"Yeah. So what?"

"Well in something like Lawrence Welk music, you get no left hand. It thumps along ok, but you don't get any variation, improvisation. . ."

"Improvisation! Dad, where'd you pick this stuff up?"

"Ken Trainor. Remember him? . . . Well I am learning. I play some now, keyboards and computer if you can believe that . . . . But anyway, that's what separates a good player from an average one, what he can do with his left hand. Art Tatum, listen to him sometime."

"Okay."

"The point is, your mother is a great right hand. She soars, can get lyrical with her life, take off and do stupid things, but I can't hold that against her, can't you see that? Heck, I drove her to half of it."

"And you're the left?"

"In a way. I'm steadier in some ways, but I feel like I've got to keep up my end now and do some of my own stepping at the same time. In a different way. I can stay still too. Moreso than she can probably. But my point is, that's what we are together: music, you know, if I play. A good music . . . Of course, I don't clean up the kitchen like I should when she's gone, but I'm working on that. I'm her stake in the ground . . . . she needs that."

"I guess, Dad. But don't you need the same mind to make good music?"

"Depends on who's doing the playing."

"Geez, you sound like Mary."

"I've been meaning to ask you about that."

Keith mailed in his forced resignation without much fanfare and just said that he couldn't continue after everything that had happened. He wanted to get on with his life. Katie was silent at first; that was a lot of money to turn one's back on. But she said, finally, shaking her Evangelical head, that the whole scene had gotten to be too much for everyone. Besides, she pointed out, giving him a hip as he walked by, she had cookies to bake.

Keith and his father spent more and more time together, fishing and tinkering in Gerry's shop. They got interested in restoration projects and found a great '68 MGA Roadster. They spend a good two months on it. And soon enough they had a small extra business on the side: fixing up jeeps. They'd take them to four wheel mud races where Keith could keep the competitive edge he had gotten so used to over the years.

They put up a hand-lettered sign—even though Keith had money to burn, Gerry insisted that they stay small potatoes. He'd spent a goodly number of years building up a local clientele, and he didn't want to change that now by using a lot of polish and chrome. And though he wouldn't admit it, Keith liked that. Dad was still Dad.

Icons and vigil lights illumined the corners of their small 3-bay garage, and Keith insisted that they stop work each day at 3 to say the Divine Mercy Chaplet and Rosary together; he took to wearing the "Our Lady of the Outfield" medal his father had forged. (Second base hidden behind her, first and third, lined, on either side beneath her outstretched arms, a glove and crossed bats beneath her feet.)

You could find the two of them rolling under jeeps during busy months, making time to go to Keith's races. The younger couple, almost of one mind by this time, would travel to shrines throughout the world or work in soup kitchens during the slower months. Julia took up Real Estate part time, and Katie went back to school, decided that she wanted to do some distance ed., an M.A. in theology from the Franciscan University of Steubenville.

As it turned out Gerry got Keith interested in music and bought him a hammered dulcimer. Keith delighted in spending his spare time in his own modest newly built house banging away in the attic. In time, he got Katie to accompany him to festivals, take up the fiddle.

They had another son, whom they named Tyrone Jacobs Malamud Wells. And though no one encouraged the little guy, in a few years he took to carrying a stick around the house, hitting a ball at every opportunity. Grandpa would pitch to him, and to the amazement of nobody, he was a natural.

IV.

Money:

Miracles. Apparitions. Mary or Satan himself. How was I to know about either? I was not Catholic, have not become one. I'm a sportswriter, plain and simple, though I must admit that what I've seen come down these last months falls well beyond anything I can explain. I saw three people actually grow eyeballs in their heads: from milky white soup to clean blue irises, just like that. A snap of the fingers. But I've seen other things too. I've seen Indians Park, a beautiful $250,000,000 edifice, reduced by the singing of jackhammers to nothing as well; I've seen the integrity of a game I love go up in holy smoke.

Finally it's all over, thank—who can use the word—God. We're finally back to where we belong: the sports pages, hem-lines, baseball.

It was a long time coming. For awhile there, some serious questions were being raised about the viability of the season itself, the town's image as a Major League venue. We had seen the infield reduced to a revival tent show, a healing circus; we'd seen an entire stadium destroyed, carried off in a hundred different directions, as relics (if you can believe that). We'd seen a perfectly normal community thrown off kilter, possessed by a kind of medieval religious mania. Many people were healed as well, of course; there's no denying that, and we're all grateful. But in retrospect don't we have to ask ourselves some pretty hard questions here, really, questions about cost, about lifestyles, about what matters?

Was it all worth it?

As it turned out, it WAS a great season, a World Championship season. The one we've all so patiently waited for this last half century. And yet, even in its wake, who around here can get the accompanying insanity out of his or her mind? The two are so bound up in memory, in that summer, that no one can think of one without the other.

Just to give you an idea of how crazy things got, let me run this column I wrote in late August by you. The stadium was just beginning to crumble as hawkers of all sorts jammed into the concourse; the police by this time, having been reduced to near bystanders. I called the column "The Other Games People Play":

> Call it a scattering of money-lenders. Call it "what comes around." But whatever you do, don't call me in for dinner. Like most of you, I've got to see how this movie ends.
>
> Yesterday, on the stadium concourse, we saw two, count 'em, two sets of tables overturned, two kinds of commodity brokers given the bum's rush—and the metaphysical implications were staggering. The first set to go were third world "cash in on the proceedings" types, most of them named Ahkeem or Akmed. They got chased from this secular temple by feminists in jack-boots who had come to demonstrate and who weren't about to be put off by a bunch of uncomprehending post-colonialist chicken salesmen.
>
> But chicken salesmen who come 3,000 miles to hawk their wares do not leave easily. Or so it would appear. And their would-be feminist mentors soon left in an even bigger hurry, chased from their own tables as Moslem brothers, veiled sisters mounted a counter-attack, knives in hand, routing those who would save them from their Patriarchal yoke.
>
> One should have to pay to see these things.
>
> But then again, perhaps we have. After all, what were we watching here, comedy or tragedy? Was there any difference? To those of us who love baseball this whole season is becoming more tragic by the minute. We're seeing the game we love tramped by religious, and other feet.
>
> But for those who have a "higher" calling, this may be what the real Doctor has ordered. Who am I to say, maybe the pointy-headed intellectuals are right. Maybe this whole circus IS still

just a case of one religious line, a Judeo-Christian-Moslem one, attempting to displace pagan others, the fourth quarter of an intense Tigris-Euphrates versus the land of Ur playoff game that began some 5000 years ago.

But even THAT is only one reading. Some members of the religious pompadour right, for example, insist that this is only a two minute drill, a grandstand effort on the part of ecclesial types who would use fear and spectacle to try to turn back the clock, to put us all at the mercy of a steeple-hatted, white-clad foreign despot.

And there are others, even farther out. Some of my personal favorites: 1) psychic ruptures in the collective unconscious, 2) a stone in God's shoe, 3) unusual galactic configurations, and 4) Gaia's motherly attempt to warn, heal her wayward children. (Some have even taken to whirling dervishly on the steps of City Hall—for some reason).

In any case, until they eventually got the National Guard gate, the unconcerned up-front Mid-Easterners were much-needed comic relief in the face of all the madness that was still going on on the field. They unashamedly argued, after all, in true time-honored American/Wall Street fashion over foreign currency on a crumbling stadium's concourse, surrounded by the clicking of thumb cymbals, the squawking of live chickens. It was a metaphor that didn't have to be one: life's real and true bazaar.

What seems especially ironic to me here, though, is that unlike the earlier market and temple scene (circa 33 A. D.), these dove salesmen weren't given the bum's rush by the whips of patriarchal Virtue, or even by tactful owners—though if you remember, they did have the first crack at it. No, the most vocal naysayers were, oddly enough, a different kind of Messiah: the culture police, Big Sister and the company she was holding (perhaps hostage).

To the women-in-question's credit, however, they did manage to talk with Peter Jennings on the evening news. You'll be able to see their placards, their cries for justice no doubt for the next week in the privacy of your own living room: "We don't want your heaven," "Give us women priests." But in forcing a confrontation, they revealed their weakness. They could not, in baseball parlance, put up the numbers.

It was the Pirates against the '27 Yankees all over again, any defense against Joe Montana as people just keep pouring into the Park on crutches, home-made stretchers, looking to be

> patched up, apparently ignorant of their more profound victimhood.
>
> And much as I miss baseball, there is a certain satisfaction in that.
>
> But as to the bigger issues: who's finally right here, who will win out, I couldn't say. Ask me about earned run averages, about the good old days when Ernie Banks wanted to play two, when Honus Wagner would go out in uniform after the game and throw the ball around with the kids. Now THAT, I'm sure, would have made God, if She ever existed, smile.
>
> (Oh, by the way, the Tribe won in 11, 3-2.)

Like an old, valued bad habit or the cousin who won't go away, the more traditional money-lenders have, of course, finally returned, selling over-priced memorabilia. Just as they did, I'm sure, that first time in Jerusalem. Things are as they were before the apparitions, the healings started. The new season will begin shortly; the fans will come back, eventually to a new stadium. But besides that, has anything been changed? A constrictive past, warm and miraculous though it was, held sway for a summer in our media lives. Everyone wanted, for that time, to become a priest. But do those warm fuzzies ever last? Haven't the strident voices of the "better truth" come back again, making their bitter sense, trying once again to out-shout the blasts from a rigid past, a perhaps dying religion?

But, then again, journalism is not about truth, he said; it's about stories.

And let me tell you, there were plenty of those to go around last year: stories about people being healed, or better, stories about the few NOT being healed; stories about the first local pennant race in 50 years. Each one of them, once-in-a-life stories, with "Award Winning" written all over them. One by one they came up like hanging curves, each smiling in succession on its way to the plate. All we writers had to do was follow through, watch the big flies for a moment, their majestic clean arc reach into the night before we began our calculated trots, shortening our steps like Ricky Henderson or Albert Bell as we approached each base. And we weren't alone in elevating our slugging percentage; the team, forever doormats and also-rans, was finally, in our lifetimes, actually winning big.

But all that's history. All that's left of the place now, five months later, is a hole, some rubble, (and I don't mean Barney, for those of you out there with low foreheads, balding feet). By the time the hordes of Medieval gleaners finish with the place, there will be nothing left. Maybe a piece of rebar poking up somewhere, maybe a few splinters, something for future gleaners. And then, by all accounts, a chapel. All of the original park, a holy relic—much of it undoubtedly to show up on the black relic market.

(The whole scene reminds me of an imagined incident a Catholic reporter told me about: a fan had bitten off the toe of St. John of the Cross as she kneeled to kiss the dead Saint's remains back in 1591. He imagined the accused confronted, responding in mumbles: "Wha toeu? Wwho mwe? Noeuw." The side-long glances, shake of the head, the mouthed insistence as she backed toward the door.)

The point is, what COULD one do but laugh? Even if this WAS baseball, and a pennant stretch run at that. The whole thing had gotten so crazy that game times had to be radically altered during an early September homestand. The league office was fit to be tied and called Nancy, had to rummage for a face to put on the whole thing.

By the time the smoke had cleared this fall, the place looked like Vonnegut's Dresden; you couldn't even tell base paths had been there. Just that trickle of water, coming up from nowhere, right behind where second base, grass had been, where Wells had ranged.

By late November, pilgrims had begun circling the place which was rapidly becoming only the bones of a stadium, pocked beyond repair. And on the surrounding streets, the crunch of chickens, just some pin feathers in the red mesh, caressed by the seasonal powdery ribbons of snow snaking out on Carnegie, Ontario. Stretchers and crutches were actually piled twelve feet high outside, litters, frozen, made the sidewalks impassable. Bandages blew down the street, like stiff pennants in a freezing breeze.

Perhaps that gauze was simile: America, like Lazarus, being raised. What had she called it? The culture of death, the institutionalization of evil? Maybe these were its bandages, one by one, being loosed. Wells certainly wanted to believe as much, but his hope may have eclipsed his sight on that count. If you don't believe me, try to walk down Upper St. Clair alone some night.

Finally the health department came to the rescue, dressed in tax dollars: new white moon suits, took all the disease away and burned it. By December there were wrecking crews.

Was all of this some Divine apocalyptic statement? Did the Virgin Mother, if that's what she was, pick such a public place because the end, as she has reportedly said, is getting terribly close? Maybe, but the thing that is hard to understand is does she really think that people becoming Catholic is going to change anything? We live on dirt, after all, not in heaven. We've got our jobs to do, our bills to pay. We're mostly everyday stiffs, not Mother Theresas. Most of the people I know recycle, are basically high-minded. Most do what they can.

But, ah, "Will you have done enough," the preacher asketh? (Put thy money in the basket.)

There may be answers to these questions. And perhaps more importantly, questions to those questions. But you can grow old, lose your sight splitting all those hairs. It's almost spring after all, and as everybody who knows anything knows, that means baseball, with a capital B, and that rhymes with Edward G., see? All of it right here in River City. It's time to shake the cobwebs, darn it; it's time to celebrate the deaths of some unendangered species: cows and horses, trees; it's time to break out the gloves and balls, the bats.

It all started, the Year of the Holy Championship, in the usual way, a whole line of February pitchers, the boys of our summers: the cracking of successive catchers' mitts. Like fireworks they signaled our revived hopes. Coaches hovered around those arms like Mrs. Adams, my third grade penmanship teacher, giving tips: come down over the top, pull it down like a shade; don't throw across your body, finish your cursive strokes. And the faces, younger each year, were, as they are every year, earnestness itself. (Most soon enough bound to busses, to places like Canton, Kingston, Columbus, Buffalo.)

Reporters re-enacted the usual rites, standing, rutting around the batting cage, (Stravinsky would've been proud) trying to get the skinny. Did this guy's arm have another year in it? Could we unscrew it, have a look? Did anyone else hear those violins? Had the off-season done anything for that one's head? And what exactly were we going to do for a lefty set-up man, order, in all this music anyway?

Managers and coaches carried on business as usual, doing their best Pattons. Listening to them, you'd think this all actually MEANT something in a world of matronly religious harangues, terrorism: right wing extremists, skin heads.

But maybe, just maybe, if one doesn't go overboard, baseball does have a small place in our lives for precisely those reasons. A useful, if not very important distraction. And there IS drama, human drama in it. Dramas with all the real and symbolic tragedies of any staged performance anywhere. Cheap ones, heroic ones. It's all there, all of it in some small way useful if one doesn't lose perspective.

And that's where we come in, vying for your time, your common dime. And if some of our guild take our task too seriously, see themselves as cultural road warriors, trying in some way with good writing to mend what the public school system has rent, most of us are simply doing our jobs, pointing out as rationally as possible, the oddments, the small victories, injustices along this route.

Take this year. There are worthwhile stories. Can the pitching staff, George Romero's undead, for example, do it again? I mean, how COULD they—that eye-popping 2.78 collective ERA, all those heroics? How will they even be able to match the competitive level of their opponents, given all the distractions? Will they, in other words, be able to deal with success?

The whole town's still on that wagon, of course, even if the wheels are beginning to wobble. Who wouldn't be? They've even over-taxed themselves to help the Jacobs' insurance company build ANOTHER new stadium. Advance sales are way up, even with Beto, Wells, gone, the games being played over in Buffalo for most of the season. They liked feeling so holy, I suppose, rooting for their chosen team, basking in the fleeting Motherly sunshine of complete victory. We all did.

But as that road north, that holy season of memory drew near, we could hear the clock ticking. The locals had been a good team; that was no revelation. They'd been second best for two years in a row. But would they be good enough to get over that final hurdle? Small markets, after all, only get a brief window of opportunity—if they get one at all (think of David Sterns and the bent Patrick Ewing envelope).

But even if we didn't have ratings power, we did have some pretty impressive numbers. Most of the team had put them up the year before. Just a bit more pitching and we might be seeing late fall games, after all these years, our breath in our faces. And so we writers gingerly rode and coaxed the crest of two point seven million dreams, crushing peanut after peanut in our nervous hands, talked in semi-serious, almost reverential tones. We walked around the players as if they were made of porcelain, as if our too heavy step would shatter what we will never be able to hold.

Like most writers, I stretch the truth if I have to on a given day. So far on some days that it would cry out "uncle" were I to give it voice. I make ordinary feats seem extraordinary, create Rocky Balboas, only to harpoon the characterization as I do so. I try to put together something to keep folks from thinking too much about the day ahead, something to go with that first cup of coffee. Besides, fictions are the perfect medicine here where cartoon characters think themselves real, speak of themselves in third person.

And personally, because the hopes WERE so high, I must admit I held nothing back. We were only a half step away, and our larger-than-life heroes were going to take that step, dammit. And Howie Freize, the skip, (who came up with that title any way, a Scandinavian named Wally Cleaver?) agreed with me apparently, because he came into opening day swinging, waging a battle with clichés. (They were his friends, winning.) This year we wuz going to do it. Climb the mountain, swim the sea, beat the damn Yankees, finally be free.

Veteran players, however, like Wells, yawned and scratched in all the usual places. They'd heard, seen all this before: seasons, kids who started out like comets, only to settle into an asteroid belt: cold, blue—and in a puff of moon dust, gone. They came and went, as they do every year, these phenoms, sent down while the tested warmed to the task at hand.

Whatever his personal problems, Beto seemed his usual self that spring, laughing, taking his usual extra infield practice. The other players liked him. Everybody did. He wore his cap rally-style when the situation demanded, could play a first rate practical joke. Last year his best involved two rookie Hispanic players: Tavares and Ramirez, in Florida. He arranged to have the immigration police come into the clubhouse, warrants in hand, cuff the unsuspecting babes, escort them in rude fashion to their cruisers. The guys could hardly speak English, had no idea, began to panic.

Everybody rolled. It was funny, in a very sick baseball sort of way, granted, but I ask you, does that sound like the behavior of a saint? That was the odd part. He was a good guy, a fine player, but there was nothing obviously virtuous about the guy. I don't know if he even went to church much early on. Oh, on some days you could find him hanging with the Bible readers, but then on others, he'd snarl at reporters—all lambs, if the truth be known—stop talking to us altogether.

We all knew there was some minor strain at home. But that's not so unusual in this business, what with the travel, the groupies. So what was the story then? Had he been unstable all along, and was only now beginning to lose his grip? Maybe, though his boyhood seemed normal enough, at least from what I could glean. No pentagrams or cleanly incised farm animals. Slightly above average as a student, in a laid back Northern California way.

But even if he were in his own peculiar left field, does mass hallucination, hypnotism, or the creative visualization account for 1,328 M.D. and M.S. patients cured in one afternoon? Rows upon rows of them in concentric circles, having responded to the announcement, straightening right out, getting out of their wheel chairs, spittle no longer a problem, their dancing, now a joy, not some grotesque commentary on God and the universe. Each case documented by a medical professional.

Who can say? I can't account for an atom of that, or anything else for that matter. Maybe it was a Catholic miracle; maybe it WAS some kind of cosmic rupture; maybe all the planets four galaxies over suddenly stopped and had tea; maybe I caused it by tearing off my left thumbnail.

It happened. What else can you say?

And what was truly remarkable about all of this was that Wells had his best year. He was the team catalyst. His average, always very good, was a career best: .341, with 112 RBIs, 15 homers. He took his usual chances on the bases, had 70 SBs. Plus he had that maniacal fire of his; he would routinely kick the ball out of second basemen's gloves; he led the league in scowls, HBPs, sprints down to first. All from a number two hitter. He made it happen.

(Maybe he should have offered a seminar in apparitions before he retired.)

The regular season itself began with a bang, only to get better. The troubled Featherheads of erstwhile times had for the first time in memory gone into the Bronx and come out wearing new war paint, beating a new drum. They'd swept four from the hated New Yorkers, and never looked back—much. It was like a breath of fresh Spring air for all of us.

We all wanted to be delivered from second place, and this was an early indication that it might finally happen. Of course the look of newly cross-cut grass, temperatures hot enough to bring out tank tops and shorts didn't hurt either. But whatever the reason, we beat-writers felt like we could finally immerse ourselves in the luxury of possibility again as we kicked back with colleagues and beers, engaged in spirited conversation on warm nights, starlings swooping in the outfield at dusk after gnats.

We charted our pitches like we did every year, razed the spread of cold cuts, olives, pastries between innings with our usual gusto, but there was a warmer glow there, even early on. People who hadn't spoken to each other for years found quips, themselves being slapped on the back.

The team, defending champions, will soon start the season playing out of town. Will there be any more miracles up anyone's sleeves, heavenly or otherwise? I think we can assume that God still likes baseball, the Indians. She did say, jesting, Wells told some intimates, that it WAS good. It was where she said she'd heard most of the praying going on in the city, Sunday afternoons in the fall. (And who exactly were the Denver Broncos?)

But she's left the home team, stopped appearing, and even if pilgrims still occasionally march around what's left of the place, it's clear that for the rest of us, some of the holy wind has gone out of our sails.

It's almost as if the whole community labored too much to image it, make it happen. And what could any of us do to follow up that season anyway, even if we felt we could control things enough to make that possible? It'd be like following Mae West on stage, Barry Manilow or Beethoven the dog.

But she WAS right. It IS good. It's time-honored, aesthetically pleasing, a link to our younger days, a hope for the ones to come. Why shouldn't it keep its revered place in our lives? Anyone who ever went to the old Municipal Stadium with Dad, warmed to the smell of cheap cigars, urine, who ever heard the endless talk of trader Lane: Coleman for Temple, Cash for Demeter, Colavito for Kuenn, Gordon for Dykes, Maris for Power, who ever helped carry a cooler, butter-stained grocery bags full of popcorn knows what I mean. It comes back, for all of us.

To the young it offers a field to test themselves, and for the rest of us, nostalgia. It reminds us of what we've lost, suggests, maybe, how we might get it back again. That certain childlikeness, innocence. All of it, only a game away.

Though that's only half of it, of course. To be honest, it was a way out of innocence as well. Remember when you were a kid, and the rain'd be coming down, moderately outside on the morning of the day you were supposed to play. Like kids everywhere, you'd sit by your window, just suffer. "God, please make it stop raining by this evening. I'll be a better person; I'll be a priest if it stops raining. . . . Maybe it'll slow down. . . . The clouds look like they're breaking over that way. . . . Maybe the coach will bring some rakes and a shovel like last time; we'll be able to fill in the batter's boxes, dry it out with sand, enough for a game to start anyway. . . . We can pitch from in front of the mound, hurry on and off."

But then the rain would get heavier, your prospects as well.

What else could you do in your uniform but pound the ball, harder and harder into your Billy Pierce glove, flop back on your bed, wonder if there were anything else really worth doing in this world?

A cold lesson in detachment.

We used to wear those sticky polyester uniforms when I first started playing all those years ago. We'd wait out in the muggy, polyester-sticky infield in our new tight red shirts, the lettering and numbers sticking to your skin from the inside (no t-shirt underneath), in jeans, the caps we hadn't learned to curl yet, wait for our turn, groundballs under threatening clouds. One lollipop after another, the ball around the infield. I'd try to get into the hum of things, punch my tiny fist into my oversized mitt. All that childhood hope.

My managers were always oafs. Everybody's must have been. They didn't know much of anything, about baseball, about life, but they COULD rub spit into their palms, pound that ball into the dirt, making the obligatory mistakes: balls lined over infielders' heads, no one out there to back up. They lived, or so it seemed, to re-experience their own glory, all of it real, if imagined.

These guys were supposed to lead us! I was amazed, even back then, though I probably couldn't have articulated why. The politics of a beer-drinking, perhaps, working class neighborhoods where some guy'd be challenged after talking too loudly, too long. He'd be our coach.

I'd be out there with the rest of the little farmers, pounding my glove like there was no tomorrow. My first was a firstbaseman's. My Dad had gotten it a few years before from Vic Power, and it was, no exaggerating, half my rather diminutive eight year old size. I had to hold it up with my off hand. But there I'd be, waiting for my ground ball, my chance to do a Kubek, take my first apple.

I suppose like all of us, I wanted to make my Dad proud, do what he never could. All of us, entrusted with the mission. Make it right kid. Make it. And why not? It made for bonding if nothing else, a whole new generation some time later at another bar, every one of them, potential managers.

It makes you wonder how long this has been going on. Adam probably couldn't hit the curve, passed the baton on to Cain who struck Abel with it because HE could.

When I first saw Wells there praying, it was like most May days that year: blue, sunny, hot. I came out early, as I often did, set my tanning tin under my chin in the high mezzanines. And there he was, on the field, long before anyone else, kneeling with his beads, his hands raised behind second base. Kneeling for God's sake. He was lucky he was there early, I remember thinking. He would've been laughed to scorn had any of the other players been around.

V.

It was the summer of our lives. One that, all things considered, we'll not see the likes of again. And even if Richard III, out of New York, still had his dollars and his hunchback; his gruesome jig, for at least one year, was up. He had pitched more money at his problems than the Federal Government, wheeled and new dealed to the winter of his discontent, made all the more glorious by the still-to-come autumn sun in New York. It would shine, after all, on a sullen Mr. Baseball, Steinbrenner, the man who's done more to harm the game than any single individual since a fellow New Yorker named Rothstein.

He turned up ex-drug addicts, boozers, female impersonators, a circus clown, but none of it helped. For this one year, there WAS justice in the world; for this one year, greed didn't pay. Casey was dead, Mickey and Whitey were probably still in the same bars, but their playing days were over. It was OUR turn, darn it.

Even those long in the trenches still, a year after, go about their business at a slightly more relaxed pace around here. Bus drivers still actually wait for you, garbage men put the lids back on your cans. Cabbies open doors, will help old ladies with packages. Everyone, without a word, still shares the memory—as if speaking could only shatter the dream we tread on, as if the very act of verbalization could only sully what is too real to stay.

All of us remember last year, how you could go to any of the Metroparks, find picnic tables with complete strangers clustered around the holy monolith, a radio. Like the obelisk in 2001, A Space Odyssey, it was the true singer of our monkey dreams.

And if it's still too much a part of most of us to re-live those days so soon, given the scope of the larger picture, it's a BASEBALL STORY that has to be told.

By early May, the temperatures around here were already in the 80's. And it would only get hotter. By July1st the mercury reached 94 degrees, and the Indians were in first place. Like Hardy's twain, fate had decreed a convergence: the elements, both natural and supernatural, and baseball. And like anything titanic, the predestined players in question had a grandeur as they moved, inextricably to their—I have to say it—destinies.

It had become too hot to breathe. Beaches, crowded before they were officially opened, now became as clogged as L. A. rush hour traffic. You couldn't find a place to put your towel, and the wavering heat, singe of sand, exacted high tolls. And the top rung of the League ladder was just as crowded. The Indians, the White Sox, the Yankees. Something would have to give.

And though the White Sox were the first to blink, they weren't the only ones who would wilt under all that heat. Like flowers gone limp, people were down to their last petals all over town. Scuffles erupted at stop lights, in bars, at work. Usually amenable wives were now quick with supper, plates like large coins, spinning on the table. Blind people hit their dogs.

Bay Village, usually a sleepy little suburb, was a perfect example. Nothing ever went wrong here. Kids played little league every evening until darkening lake water, washing up on finally cooling beaches, lulled them and any boogie who may have been disturbing them, to sleep. At least in most cases.

Marilyn Seltzer was the exception. In the words of my good friend Mushy Wexler: "She didn't sleep so good that night." The next sunny suburban July morning she woke up to was somewheres else. With, one would presume, a rather substantial headache. Her husband, Dr. Samuel Gerber Seltzer, plastic surgeon to the stars, had, without further consultation, attempted to re-arrange her features the night before. All done in a slightly more elementary fashion than had heretofore been his want. And with only one instrument, a blunt one.

He claimed, of course, that he had been knocked out, wore a neck brace for weeks to prove it. But it wouldn't wash, despite the parade of Hollywood elite that the defense kept trotting out as, go figure, character witnesses. He had money, style, all the things that interest us. But old mo wasn't in his corner either. It only had a towel for our DA, one Shondor Eberling.

The trial was good theater, lasted throughout the summer, provided some needed interludes from more pressing spherical and religious matters. And that was providential. Before long, too many of us would be fastening our safety belts for what would prove to be a very bumpy baseball night.

The Wahoos beat the hated Pale Hose on the third, using three pitchers to come one out short of fireworks, a perfecta. It was a sign of near perfect things to come as the homeboys would go into the All-Star break on a tear, feasting like good young black directors at the box office. Philadelphia, Baltimore, Washington: they were second division meat, and like extras in a movie about the hood, lay strewn all over the infield. Those who hadn't died succumbed to the culture of victimhood, went crawling for cover as the Indians got plenty busy, rolled up a 40-8 record against them in a bum's rush, and it was only the first half of the season.

On July 13th, the All-Star game was played before a sell-out crowd at the Park, four of the town's idols in the starting line up. Rosebud, our MVP third sacker from the year before (he'd come one percentage point short of the triple crown), clubbed two home runs and a single, had 5 RBI's. Beto knocked in two runs to tie the game in the eighth, and Peoples came off the bench and smacked a pinch-hit homer to win it in the ninth.

If the off-time was supposed to provide a breather from the seasonal wars, no one in this town felt it, at least for the duration of the game. I DO suspect, though, that if you listened closely that night, you might've heard a collective sigh, a pause, a pleasant inhaling. The time it took to light up Auerbach cigars, all over the city. It was going to be that kind of summer. Not for those with weak constitutions maybe, but a summer to celebrate nonetheless.

Change was in the air. You could feel it. And if further proof of that fact was needed, it came soon enough, though not all of it was relegated to the corner of Carnegie and Ontario.

Because it was the summer, too, of Woody Woods, a college golfer who had won the U. S. Junior the year before, taking center sports stage, vying for the U. S. Amateur. No one had ever won both. Woody was special; his very presence was like a one man consciousness-raising seminar. He was multiculturalism in the very flesh, come down like the Huns to sweep the staid, lily white decadent golfing world of antiquity off its feet. One quarter Thai, one quarter Chinese, one quarter Afro-American, one eighth American Indian, one eighth white, he would take the Augusta overflow crowd with him as he charged through the back nine as if he were the scourge of God. Bob Sweeney, his opponent in match play, never had a chance.

The timid called it class war, as he had grown up in the hills of Western Pennsylvania, worked for his Dad who was handyman and groundskeeper, a small-time pro. Some, a little more direct, called it "the only race war worth winning." Whichever it was, it was damned good golf, and damned good to see. Just about everybody cheered, too, especially here, where the whole town wore Chief Wahoo on its sleeve.

Whoever said what is worth having is worth struggling for must have been a baseball fan. By July 22nd, the Gotham Bullies had won 10 in a row, 23 of their last 30. Their dollars were showing. They had purchased some heavy lumber midseason, and the big, slow-footed oafs were beginning to jell. And even though the Indians were still going well themselves, 10-3 since the All-Star break, our heroes could hear footsteps. The Yanks had done them one better, going 12-2.

If collisions have foreshadowings, we all could feel them. But the questions was, were we the Titanic or were we the iceberg? The first indication came on a trip to the Apple. The

Indians put their feet down for what they hoped would be the last time on John Wayne's throat, took three out of four.

But the scourge of recent and long-term memory would not go away. As July seared itself into history, the home team began to fumble with a new sensation: first place in August, as if it were a hot potato. They weren't used to the heat that came this late in the season. And they weren't the only ones. Local beaches had to be closed because of the sweltering polluted haze. There were several power outages; more than a few elderly people died in their closed-up apartments. THE PRESS did what it could: printed the usual photos, an egg frying on the sidewalk, opened fire hydrants. But first place in the pitiless gaze of an August sun? No one knew what to expect, heard only the reeling birds. The players, the fans, we had no experience.

The Yankees, however, did. They were out to make it 6 world titles in a row, and years of dogfights had taught them to unhinge their jaws, seize a foreleg when an opening came. It came. Certainly not to our surprise. All we could hear in our mind's ear was the crumpling of bulkheads. Whifty Schmitt, an iceberg if there ever was one, threw a 4-hitter at the Tribe, leaving 43,000 sad patrons, painted faces, the bare letter-chested to cross downtown streets, heads bowed, every imaginable type of tomahawk, dejectedly at their sides.

Would it happen again the populace wondered? Later than usual, but would it happen? How many times could Casey strike out, or strike us out, anyway? How many seasons could be blown before we as a collective would stop investing our time and money, our dreams on fine summer Friday evenings, take our children to watch the carnage? How many times would we take the trains home, cars of sullen emptiness bouncing on rough tracks, too defeated to enjoy the blessings of a warm night?

It was the specter of all the seasons past, bringing with them the chains of summers ill-spent. "Ebineezer (or James). You have wasted your life." It was our dark night. Would we have the answer this time? Would we ever have the answers? Would the team wake up the next day, look fate in the eye and spit, or would we die the death we'd come to accept as our very own?

Beto spat. He passed go with a clutch three run homer. That and some excellent pitching, a ninth inning triple play were enough to put us back on an almost even keel. The ship might have been taking water, but we had plenty of bailing equipment.

We would need it. Mickey Muddle took Winn Early deep twice on Sunday, and there they were again, our worst nightmare. Like Butch and Sundance's Pinkertons, they were unhurried, sure as the signs in the dust. We could've asked "Who are those guys?" but we knew. It had become painfully clear for all of us. We might be able to end this movie for a year, if we were lucky, but they would be back. As long as there was baseball, we would never be able to end the show.

They would be back the next year, and the next. They would be back when our children outgrew us, became little league managers. And they would smile then, too, a symbol for all we can never own: the finish.

They must've leaned some in their saddles as they rode away that day. Only a game and a half back, they had every reason to be confident. They'd been down this road before.

But larger forces intervened. Though the results of that intervention wouldn't show for awhile. The home team, in the duration, kept on plugging, won games on the 11th, 12th, 13th, 14th, and two on the 15th. The Yankees, another name for surety, quietly won 7 to our 6 in the same time span.

Some fans got desperate, went on vision quests, fasted, said rosaries, did Billy Jack snake dances. Did it help? Who could say? The locals did manage ten in a row before feeling the miles and trials, losing one on an error in the ninth. The Yankees responded, winning 11 straight. Still, their streak wasn't enough, wasn't to be. Within two weeks, just before the Bombers were scheduled to come and raze our town, the Tribe caught a second wind, won 7 in a row to the Yanks 6.

It was September by then, and the perennials would need a three game sweep just to keep the pressure on. And they got it, despite some great individual play on the part of Beto, Peoples. But something QUIETLY miraculous happened.

There was no empty silence this time, no collective sigh of despair. The worst HAD happened; we had taken their best shot, and we were still taking air. Our houses, our children were safe. We were still 3 1/2 up with only the second division left to play. That breeze out on the lake, strong enough to generate small-craft warnings, wasn't a sigh of relief. It was a yawn! With less than a month to go and only two more head-to-head meetings, we had 'em. Everybody knew it. We had 'em.

Oh sure, the Indians had to handle the bums, but they had done that all season. And to no one's surprise, the trend continued. On September 6th, they tied Tris Speaker's 1920 World Champions' record: 98 victories. On the 7th they broke it. Nobody minded the record hot weather; it only gave folks more reason to find the virtue in hops, barley, to take that extra dip in the neighborhood pool, swimming hole. The town swayed, gleefully in the heat. We had been through crescendo; now it was decrescendo, with the swaying of steins, 2 a.m. dancing on the streets in the Flats. We had, at last, my brothers and sisters, done it.

Of course, THEY came again, on September 12th. But no one around town was worried. Even though the Yanks were on a pace to win 105 games, the venerable ones would fall short if they couldn't sweep, get some major help. It was not forthcoming.

They ate dirt. And the Indians took no prisoners; they took, instead, hair: 4-1 and 3-2. On the 17th, the home team was officially in, won their 106th game, and on the 25th won game number 111, breaking the winning percentage mark of the '27 Yankees.

And that rattling? Was it the Babe's bones as he rolled over in his grave. Maybe. But I don't think so. Take a close look at those old photos. Tell me you can't see some Indian in the man. Then what was the sound? A hollowed, beaded and beating gourd of a local medicine man, somewhere down Lorain Ave., giving thanks for things finally set right.

The World Series was anti-climactic, really. The Yokohama Giants had a good team, but we were on a roll.

Four straight. It was too bad, Willie Mays Hays' fibula. But even if he had caught that ball, you can't tell me it would have made any difference.

That was the baseball part of it. It deserves its own space. The other story I kept under wraps as long as I could. It seemed like a such a personal thing, and as long as it remained that way, I didn't want to interfere. But it was such an unusual display as well, early on; I had to watch, undetected.

He'd come every time, early, fall to his knees. Then one day I heard, saw something, or thought I did. A crackle of light or a humming sound. Or maybe, like most of the people who would eventually show up, I didn't SEE anything. Maybe I wanted to see something so badly, find some meaning in the hollowness of life that I thought, for a moment, that I did. That's how it all starts, no? Then, after we've convinced ourselves, we try to convince others. That's called TV evangelism. And while everybody knows that's where the money is, the journalist in me wanted to proceed cautiously. The mind, after all, is a great and wonderful thing, a magician really; it can offer healings, answers, its own heavens and hells.

But then players in significant numbers started joining him. I had to open that rather substantial can of worms; it couldn't be helped. It would either be me or someone else, and I wasn't about to lose out to some pup from the Lorain Journal.

He'd be out there each day for between eighteen and twenty minutes; then he would jerk his head up, look skyward. His whole face would change, get softer. He'd smile, move his lips. I tried to stay hidden, get a good view with my binoculars, but that was all I could see.

On one day, though, about four days into the festivities, I did see Freize and Soul, the G. M., in the dugout having a pretty animated discussion as Wells knelt out there, in holy oblivion. I discreetly cornered Soul after the game. He put on a grim face, said they were monitoring the situation, asked me to keep a lid on the story until they could figure out how to handle things, how to get Wells some help.

And help came, that was for sure. But not in the way anyone expected it to. First it was in the person of Peoples, and then Early, Houtteman, and Westlake joined in. Before too long there were ten guys out there. Now, a promise is a promise, but like I told Soul, if it went too far, it was my story. I wasn't about to lose a Pulitzer prize-winning story to anyone. So after talking to a few of the guys, finding out about the "lady," I wrote the column. And boy did the prayer books hit the fan.

The next morning about six hundred how-do-ya-do's showed up to watch. And they weren't disappointed. As Wells looked up, a gasp arose from among the faithful. People pointed. Nuns with binoculars pushed their way closer, into the box seats, enduring the occasional heckle as they did so. A lot of the people there, apparently, were regular fans, didn't know how they felt about having their space invaded. (They had no idea.) You could hear the sounds of people jumping on empty cups in the background, abusive language. It was a weird scene: someone should have been selling popcorn.

And the strangeness was only beginning. The real show started once Wells and his teammates had completed their prayers. Without enough security to restrain them, the people, like a bunch of holy autograph hounds, just poured onto the field. Most of them went after the visionary, a few oddballs taking the opportunity to race around the outfield, climb the fences.

You would have thought that Snodgrass had forgotten to touch second base or something, that Merkle had come back, dropped a fly again the way those and later fans milled about. What had she said that first crowd wanted to know. Some thrust rosaries under his nose. Would he get them blessed ? There were written requests for prayer, voices: "Remember my Aunt Ida to our Virgin Mother." Some people asked him to sign their Bibles.

He seemed genuinely surprised, said he'd take the rosaries to her, ask her about Ida. And moving quickly through the crowd, he ducked to go into the dugout, almost got hit with a flying apple. (If it was the original one none of us could ever find out.)

When batting practice began, there was little room for anybody to hit. All the players who had been there were pressed for comments. Did they see the lady? Is this the miracle it would take to beat the Yanks? Most offered no comment, except that. Westlake, speaking for the team's Bible group said that they all believed in prayer, team unity. They couldn't really tell what was happening out here, but they would stand behind Wells.

What did he think? Did he see anything? No, he didn't. But there was a tangible peace. They all believed, believed that all things were possible. Beyond that he couldn't say. Would he, Westlake, be back out there tomorrow? "No." (Laughter.)

But don't read anything into that, he said. The team was in first place, and that was their major concern. He and his teammates went out to show support, to pray for themselves and for the world. He suggested we all do the same, invited all the reporters to the Bible group they held every Friday.

To a man, the players continued in their support for Beto, even when things began to get way out of hand. And that didn't take long. When the news services got wind of the story, when the healings started, the miracle spring first sighted, he quickly became THE nightly national news visitor into 30,000,000 American homes. There were NATIONAL ENQUIRER stories, with actual pictures of the Virgin. Oprah and Sally did shows, A CURRENT AFFAIR kept close tabs on it, kept a reporter on the scene. It became a much bigger story than the pennant race, actually increased ratings. Every game, home or away, was sold out.

Hecklers wore Mary faces when he came to bat. He was shouted at by Bible-belters, feminists, all on a regular basis. I don't know how he stood up to it.

Morly Safer and Sixty Minutes showed up, 20/20 crews, foreign corespondents, each out there under bright infield studio lights to witness an apparition. A few thousand viewers called in to say they saw something. Everything from a large radish to angels surrounding Jesus' golden throne. Wells became the most talked about person in the country. But he stayed oblivious, didn't talk, just kept playing the game.

And then the first claimed healing was substantiated: a woman, who reportedly had no left eyeball, witnessed, (no pun intended) one grow in her head. Safer, in a response to a hostile pro-apparition letter, ended his show wondering about what to do with such cock-a-ma-mee stories; Hugh Downs compared the whole thing to some apparition he'd seen in Medugorje, Croatia, wondered about how much attention we should pay these things.

No cliché, metaphor was left unturned. The circus had begun with the jugglers of words leading the parade. Our own religious writer quoted Yeats: "mere anarchy is loosed," "the center cannot hold," though I never did understand what our man was referring to, the apparitions or the reaction to them. In any case, this big top would not be relegated to the playing field. Everybody wanted a piece of the holy action.

Everybody but, apparently, the local Bishop. He, a person known for his administrative gifts, was less than enthusiastic, took what he called a wait-and-see approach. But his secretary/spokesman, a priest, took to waving an Indians' pennant for subsequent press conferences, said that he, too, hoped and prayed for a pennant. Having been an Indian fan for many years, he said we certainly could use a little divine intervention around here.

Within twelve home dates, dozens of verified healings later, the stadium was packed for every game by five o'clock. Most had tickets. Others had hopped fences in the pre-dawn hours, avoided detection until the crowds got so large that they could no longer be singled out. This created security problems, of course, as many of those people didn't want to leave after the festivities, chose to mill about on the concourses, cause trouble.

But those problems turned out to be small potatoes when large scale healings started happening. People who didn't care a hoot about baseball didn't want to give up their seats, prayer spaces, for anyone. And more and more of them pushed to get in. As much as ownership tried to stem the tide, hire extra security, get people off the gates, it was a losing battle. There were just too many people.

The National Guard was called in to act as a regulating force. They checked everyone for tickets when game time came. A two ticket system was even introduced. Apparition watchers were allowed in early at a reduced price. And it all worked smoothly enough, at least for awhile. Order was restored.

But the number of healings, the crowds, just kept swelling. By the beginning of July, 150,000 per day wanted to get in, grew impatient with the sweltering heat, the ticket process. Like some huge anxious animal, the crowd rubbed its back along the gates. When it finally surged, there was little the Guard could have done to slow it down. And then after the healings, the trips to the spring, the people were so drunk with good feelings that they were in no hurry to move on, get back to their little lives with all their problems.

What could the owners, the military do, frisk and pitch 100,000 people? And what if many resisted? Were they going to use Billy clubs on pilgrims reciting rosaries? Talk about a public relations disaster. And what made the whole thing worse was the fact that many of the people milling about didn't care any more about religion than your average politician, whatever their claims to the contrary. These people were hooligans, who were only there looking for an opportunity to break a light bulb, steal some equipment.

It put the owners into a real bind, created a logistical nightmare. There were games to play, huge crowds of people to move. And the exponential growth of healings wasn't helping. Bus loads of blind people started showing up. Most of them healed, probably wanting to drive on the way home. And how was the Guard supposed to treat those sightless pilgrims, still hoping, when a game was scheduled in forty-five minutes? How would it have looked for the owners to have national news cameras showing their security guards pushing blind people around?

By early September games had to be rescheduled, some as late as 10:00 at night. Trampled, stolen sod had to be replaced every day, a missing batting cage had to be recovered. Beto did what he could, took to relaying the "Queen of Heaven's" messages at a mike that had been set up after each apparition. She asked, he said, for calm. But there were more problems as the crutches started piling up. And what about the bathrooms' waste baskets, over-brimming with diseased bandages? How could the owners expect a paying customer to go in there, risk the health of his or her children as he did so? Not so innocent bystanders brought in coolers, just to sit on, watch the proceedings amid the pleasures of beer and cold cuts. Some people set off fireworks in the middle of the crowd.

But there was no stopping it. Like a huge and efficient assembly line, people came to drink the water. Broken in, healed out. Thousands and thousands of recorded "spontaneous remissions," many times more here than at all the other apparition sights combined. And all the while, the devastation to the physical plant. Larger chunks of sod were ripped out of the outfield, rows of seats were missing, a turnstile was gone. There was graffiti everywhere.

And what's a post-Enlightenment kind of guy supposed to make of this? Were large-scale healings meant to get me to change my perspective, change all of us into medieval types, submitting to the large foreign machine? Don't get me wrong. I have nothing against Catholics, but was Wells trying to tell me that it would please the old Clock Maker if I were to, more earnestly, seek the elusive realms of mystery, perhaps take to picnicking in cowl at Stone Hedge? I don't think so. If he's up there he gave us this world to make what we can of it. We're smaller potatoes. Give me my primate brain, a few tools to dig in the dirt with. I'll consider my options, do what makes the most sense.

I've done some homework, tried to keep an open mind. Do you know how many reported apparitions of Mary occurred from 1900 until 1990? More than three hundred. And that number has increased many times over in just these last five years.

The crucial date here is 1917. Near Fatima (a nice Moslem name), Portugal, the Mother of God is proported to have prophesied before the revolution, that Russia, that little backwoods country, would spread its nasty errors all over the world, that nations would be destroyed. Okay. One for one, if the apparition did happen. A good batting average, but it was only April.

The next two apparitions seemed to have occurred in Beauraing and Banneux, Belgium, in 1932 and 33, respectively. She appeared 35 times at Beauraing, called herself "the Merciful Mother." (She should have told that to the groundskeeper's at the Park.)

All three have been approved by the Catholic Church, something that doesn't seem to happen easily when one considers how often she keeps showing up.

Jump ahead to 1961, Garabandal, Spain. Mary seems to have appeared to four mountain peasant girls. (She seems to go for peasants, simple folk in general. For their childlike simplicity or their naiveté?) During their ecstasies, the girls would freeze up into sculpture-like poses. Doctors couldn't move them. One girl received a photographed Host on her tongue, put there by an angel. And during these, Mary, if she was appearing, took up the Fatima notion of chastisement.

This is the part I just don't understand. What do these "heavenly people" expect anyway? We are humans. We like sex, money, power. It's part of who we are. Why build in an appreciation for the created world if you want your charges to deny it?

At Garabandal she is reported to have said that the "cup is filling over," that cardinals, bishops, and priest are at each others' throats, leading souls to perdition. She said there would be a celestial world-wide warning and a great miracle to be announced eight days in advance.

From there we move, in our tour, to Zeitun, Egypt, where, in an ecumenical move, she appeared above a Coptic Church. She didn't say anything for two years, '68-'70. Hundreds of thousands saw her; she was in all the newspapers. Muslims, non-believers. (One assumes the Allyotolah wasn't among them.)

Akita, Japan came next, crying statues. We've all heard about those, but this one was the ground-breaker. A statue bled human tears, blood, 101 times. (The only possible significance to that number perhaps being the Medieval gospel notion of the Lord increasing what they already have 100 fold should disciples fall in line.) The tears were tested at a Tokyo University, presumably by a believer, and were found to be of human origin. Here she picked up the chastisement theme again. "Fire from the sky," "Worse than the flood," "a great part of the world will be destroyed."

From there she took the road show to Betania, Venezuela. From 1976 until the present, she appears under the title "Reconciler of Nations." Real successful there. More than 2,000 people have seen her, none experiencing any ecstasies. This is the fourth approved citing. Not such a surprise—and please forgive me if I get out-of-bounds here— when one considers the cite. Civilization has made real in-roads in that part of the world. They expect moving pictures, running water next week.

In 1981 she appeared in Kibeho, Rwanda, Africa, kept appearing until 1989. Seven visionaries got the nod here. I find this spectacle especially interesting because here, as well as in Yugoslavia which I will get to presently, her appearance was followed by devastation, though of a viler sort than what happened at Indians Park. Not long after her "appearances," two warring tribes soon loosed themselves on each other, just as the good Catholic, Muslim and Orthodox peoples were to do in Yugoslavia.

In Medjugorje, 1981-present, Mary appears daily, no matinees, telling simple and would-be simple mountain folk to lead good Christian lives. "The cup is filling over." "Lead good lives. . . . a chastisement is coming if you do not," she says. It could be brought on my man himself.

This notion is picked up in Naju, Korea, '85-present, where Mary takes a stand against a woman's right to choose. "Fire from heaven" warnings come again.

And these are just the most famous ones. She is also appearing, for more than one time only, on international stages: in San Nicolas, Argentina, 1983; at our Lady of Lourdes Shrine in Mellaray Grotto, County Waterford, Ireland, 1985; in Inchigeela, Ireland, 1985; in Bessbrook Grotto, Ireland, 1987; in Hrushiv, Ukraine, 1986-88; in Cuenca, Ecuador, 1988-90; Litmanova, Slovakia, 1990; in Damascus, Syria, 1987; in Mozul, Iraq; in Hungary; in Escorail, Spain, 1988; in

Como, Italy, 1980-present; in Grushevo, Ukraine, 1987; and in Melbourne, Australia, 1990. There are many others as well.

Here at home she is appearing all over, in Denver, San Antonio. Every city seems to have them. In fact the expert I spoke to said that there are three in Northeastern Ohio alone: one in Youngstown, which, he says, looks pretty good, one in Seven Hills, which was new to him, and one in Carrollton, which the local bishop has asked him to investigate. He also warned me that many of these can be bogus. Witness Bayside, NY., and Conyers, Ga.

And what are daily stiffs supposed to make of this? I can't say, but I can't see her either, and that's my big problem with all of this. I don't mean to sound smart, but my job is numbers: batting averages, earned run averages, games behind, games left, how many days are left on my parking validation sticker. It's a question of did the guy make the catch or not, how much does it cost? I can try to get into a player's head for filler, but the real story is what he does on the field.

And I suspect, further, that most people are a lot like me. This heavenly person, if that's who she is, should do something that will help ME. Personally. She could clean up my arthritis, help me, and again I don't want to sound too wise, at the track. (A writer friend of mine says that she could clean up boxing. Now that would be convincing!)

The only truly amazing thing I DID see was how none of this hurt Well's production. Now that was a kind of miracle. Despite the fact that his face and his plea for old values found their way all over the Rush Limbaugh show, the national news, he never seemed to lose his foundation, kept relaying messages, getting three hits. How he managed to keep at it I don't know. Perhaps he never watched the news. God knows Rather and Brokaw found enough material there to last them for a couple of years. Both made room at the end of their programs for the latest from the apparition site. Some wacky anecdote about how the crutches were disposed of or about how beer sales have gone up at the ballyard since the apparitions started, both of them shaking their heads, leaving us with their smiles until tomorrow.

But none of it affected this guy. A Tiger second baseman, for example, threw down 50 Miraculous Medals on the field between innings one game; the Yankees put a statue of Our Lady of Perpetual Help in their dugout for one game. In Philadelphia the public announcer would pipe in Linda Blair's voice from the EXORCIST before Wells came to bat.

He stopped that pretty quickly though: three consecutive game-winning hits against them, and before you could say Harvey the Rabbit, they switched to Hildegard of Bingen, the Monks of Weston Priory.

But Wells tried to implement some hair-brained ideas, too, despite his best intentions. Trying to make some kind of religious statement, he bought whole sections for indigents, pregnant women. (How he got his hands on a whole section of tickets was miracle enough for me.) The first and only batch of the former caused all kinds of problems: there were human secretions everywhere, and stadium workers threatened to go on wildcat strike unless they got extra pay for cleaning up the urine, vomit, the excrement. There were broken wine bottles everywhere, trousers left, fights, enraged vendors, whole rows of these guys, leaving their seats for places along the bottom of the stadium concourse walls. Home, sweet home, I guess.

A few of them fell onto the playing field, one from the upper deck, dead, healed later in the vast cosmic comedy. (Let's face it. Most of us would like to do something personally for the poor, but they ARE so disagreeable, aren't they? And you'd need to carry disinfectant around with you, masks for TB, gloves for the AIDS factor. Besides, how many of them want to take responsibility, change? What good would my help be doing anyway?—Which reminds me of something I heard once from a somewhat cynical writer: why do those starving people remain on the African desert? IT'S A DESERT. Why don't they move if they want food. What do they expect there, rainfall?)

But Wells didn't have a corner on polemics. The P.C. boys and girls, or would-be boys and sometimes-girls, had to have their moments on the stage. The gay community was in quite a huff for awhile because Wells, the Lady, didn't provide a section for AIDS victims, choose to highlight their plight. One more example, they said, of the Church's homophobia. One night they acted up all over the playing field. The first few went for Wells. But the "saint," as it turned out, had not yet embraced non-violence.

The pregnant women thing might have worked, but some bright front office puppy gave them a section in the bright sun. For a whole afternoon all one saw was a series of very round women trying to run to, and clogging up, the restrooms. But as odd and potentially affirming as these happenings were, they were just the appetizers.

After word of the miraculous rate of healings got to foreign shores—pictures of the hundreds of amputees who had grown new limbs were circulated world-wide—people literally started showing up from every back water country in the world, each with his or her own customs.

What did these people know or care about baseball, a pennant race, an American game? They saw only one thing: God, on heavy Sphinx-like feet, coming again. Hundreds of Mid-Eastern folk showed up one day, setting up those tables, trying to sell incense and medals, live chickens.

And the feminists. "We don't want your miracles," "Take your heaven and shove it." They objected: this was public ground. What right did the repressive Church have in usurping the people's trust, the stadium, what right did the Jacobs have in foisting a dead patriarchy on us? They demanded equal time. Wanted to do some Wiccan rituals, goat sacrifice, put some cauldrons around second base. They wanted to put together a female baseball team.

Tables of medals, crucifixes, mideastern food were overturned in the best show of the season. Scuffles ensued, chickens flew, at least until those with the "higher" level of consciousness realized that they were outnumbered, that their enemies had knives. The latest endangered species soon ran for their lives, sought injunctions, Peter Jennings. But none of it worked. He stayed only as long as the ratings would allow him, and the courts, well, they were smart enough to move VERY slowly.

It had turned into the world's largest free-for-all. Not so bad for a writer, if you watched where you stepped. Just keep your head down and your ammo high. These stories looked like they would last forever.

But we were slow to read the writing on the walls. One morning, late in August, I came in early only to find that a huge section of the infield had been lifted. There was no grass between first and home from the line to the center of the field. What could the ground crew do? You just can't lay down that much sod and expect a team to play on it. Someone could get hurt. Perhaps the team should cancel, play elsewhere until all this blew over? But the locals didn't want to give up the home field advantage; the race was getting too tight. Finally, the General Manager, Soul, asked Wells to petition the Lady for a miracle. He did so.

The new sod rooted.

But apparently even she was limited in some way. There simply weren't enough miracles to touch some people. Despite beefed up security, good will, within three days of the sod incident, all the bats were missing, all the balls too, the left eye of Chief Wahoo was gone, and hammers and chisels had become the newest instruments of baseball torture. They sounded like chimes and echoed throughout the park. What good was a trip to the ballpark, after all, without taking home a souvenir, in this case a small holy stone?

As the trend continued, it became clear that such habits multiplied by a thousand, and daily, nightly, could have devastating effects. Huge patches of rebar began to appear. There weren't enough Guardsmen in the whole state to monitor all the people who milled and circled the stadium as if it contained the Kaaba (not a totally inappropriate image as five times a day Muslims broke out their prayer rugs on the Carnegie sidewalk outside, amid bonfires, faced East to pray).

But neither their prayers nor Mary's pleas made much of a difference. The Army would not have been able to peacefully disperse the crowds. And, in fact, the people had, for the most part, no malicious intent. Most of them were just pilgrims. They prayed their rosaries as they circled, like latter day Joshuas. And though no one doubts that their intentions were peaceful, these walls too, would answer another, if stranger, trumpet, come tumbling down.

More and more people got healed, and the rate seemed to increase exponentially as we inched our way to the pennant. A ward bussed in from a psychiatric hospital, hitched home; players on the DL from all over the league came. There were lepers, an estimated 200,000 world-wide AIDS patients. Every single person, or so it seemed, healed from August 15th to mid-September. The influx was, as you might imagine, of Biblical proportions. Some people even brought in the recently dead. And I ask you, what security guard would get in the way of that stink?

The main arteries surrounding the ballpark: Carnegie, Ontario, East 9th, Huron, and Chester were all clamped shut for 24 hours each day. Buses could no longer come into the choked heart of the city as alternate routes had to be mapped out. Who knows how many old ladies were left stranded. Businesses boomed, yes, but they had to put on more security as well; iron fences up at closing time. The mayor, ever the politician, responded to public pleas that Mary and her money leave by encouraging local churches to send down teams, be peacemakers. The national Guard, US Army did what they could as well. But how could games be played there anymore?

They did try, of course. This WAS baseball, after all, and we were in the thick of our first pennant race in decades. People wedged their way in, at 10:00 each evening, the prayer teams clearing the stadium. And we might have muddled through the rest of the season that way had it not been for the vandals. Some people soon had no seats to go to, wanted their money back. The players union questioned the safety of the conditions. For awhile it looked like the team would have to move for the remainder of the season. Finally, pressured by frazzled owners, merchants, Wells asked the Lady to desist until after the series.

And on Oct. 28th, she did so. But apparently she, too, had seen enough because the healings became much more sporadic after the season, eventually stopped altogether.

In the meantime, though, Catholics in Indian caps said vigils in thanksgiving. They were grateful for her cooperation, thanked her publicly for being such a good sport. All of it, on the local and national news. And the pocked peace remained until the season was over. Once that had been accomplished, though, Wells and his legions returned.

Like the Huns. People, at first, came back hungry. But you knew they wouldn't be satisfied with minor healings. All they had was need, and they tried to fill it first in front row seats. The Jacobs' brothers, the city, did what they could to maintain order, but more of the crowd seemed to be vandals this time around. Finally, given the rapidly deteriorating state of the stadium, the owners threw up their hands.

Healings still occurred again, but on a lesser scale. And soon the minor variety began to dominate. People got their faith back, found peace in their illnesses. Oh, there were a few good ones: hunchbacks straightened, people being cured of astigmatism. But where do you go from raising the dead? It wasn't fair. People wanted more. And finally, on one day, Wells stopped coming.

This apparently was a sign of heavenly abdication as far as the vandals were concerned. It was open season. Crowds, though smaller, grew for the most part more violent. All the gates went, one by one. Jackhammers abounded. I saw a whole team of guys, like rats, gnawing at, tearing up huge pieces of the concourse. And, no kidding, a dump truck showed up one morning at about 2:30, three guys with jackhammers, ate at the side of the building. I and the four cops next to me counted twelve men doing the loading.

Pilgrims tried to talk to the looters, pray with them, but when has that ever worked? They were pushed aside, some even beaten. And as a result of so many people having been made whole here, the building began to totter.

Finally, as I said, despite the thousands of faithful pilgrims, the city had to step in. They used the water hoses selectively, brought in the wrecking ball. For a time the mob resisted, cut hoses, pulled the operators from their machinery cabins. But with the help of the U.S. Army, tear gas, some common sense, reason finally prevailed. And within a month, all was history.

And what are we supposed to make of it, this visit from heaven on the corner of Ontario and Carnegie in Cleveland, this stream? If we are supposed to judge things by their fruits, as every good Christian will tell you, what do we see? 250,000,000 dollars worth of damage, a season almost ruined, people's annual dreams being supplanted by mass hysteria and the sound of jackhammers. Was this heaven or the heart of darkness being loosed? Was it either? Was it our dreams or our demons? Is there any difference in the end?

I saw thousands of people leave the place, changed. Many for the good. And if the cause of that is subject to some question, one can't argue with the results. But we do need to weigh things as well here, don't we? There is the all that damage; there are the heart-breaking faces of those who were not healed; there is the work of two fine, civic-minded philanthropic men destroyed.

As I say, I have nothing against Catholics, their Church, but haven't we gotten along pretty well, despite the bumps, without the Ayatollahs of this world offering us their way or the gun? And despite our wars, our stupidity, hasn't good old common sense virtue served us pretty well in our lives up until now?

Like the Yankees, reason ate, at least for a time, charred dust. But thank goodness it's back. And perhaps that is the lesson here. Whatever madness surrounds us, be it good or bad or some bizarre combination thereof, what is worthwhile survives. The next season comes. And each season, every baseball team, again, like spring, struggles to put together a winning effort, to make some good shoot happen. And it does.

The city, like the game, like us, will rebound. And if, somewhere down the line, we have to endure another bout of religious fervor, we will. Overflow crowds will fill the new stadium then too—for baseball, and the following generation's phenom will hold his first bat. Find your hope where you can. THAT is enough for me.

The series, the year, was over, and with it, the dreams we had harbored since the days of our youths. Gone. We had done it, sure. There was no denying it. We had the ring. But what do you do when you've finally gotten what you wanted, when you discover that, too, is not enough? Psychologists warn fans repeatedly about the dangers in such identification, catharsis, but it's a matter of principle for most of us, not listening to those guys. And besides, so what if we had to suffer a bit. We had kept the Yankees at bay, hadn't we, at least for one year? We could re-inflate again next year, this year.

(And what do those boneheads know anyway, those modern versions of witch doctors—the very people Arizona demands wear dunce caps with stars and a moon on them while testifying in court? Their guys never won a pennant. Their guys never won anything. They spent their best years in the basements of places like Harvard, going over dusty books, wondering why their Daddies and Mummies never loved them. Heck, I could have told them. Because they never took one for the team. Parents know that kind of stuff early.)

Yes, despite the ash and smoke out on Ontario, despite the spectacle, the home boys had done it. They'd brought home the bacon, bitten the brass ring and found out that it was made of pure gold. We did a parade just to pinch ourselves, make sure it was true. Held that trophy up high, too. Every man jack in the town were winners; we, too, just this once, could say we were the best. No one could take that away. It had been our year.

Wells is, of course, gone. And, oddly enough, despite what he brought to the team, despite his having been the catalyst, there's not a whole lot of lamentation about it. And let's face it. What he brought was too much for the common man, or woman. Most people, though they have a deep respect for religion, do not come to the ballpark to see a three-ring circus of magical healings, the work of skinheads. They do not come to see how short their own lives come when compared to heavenly things. They come to escape the drudgery of their work weeks. They come to escape. And there's nothing wrong with that.

Wells, though, wasn't built like that. He couldn't be satisfied, living in such a small ordinary world. He sought metaphors large enough to embrace his own ego. He wanted a throne. But thankfully he's gone now, gone to live in a realm worthy of his ideas: in a Winnebago, touring a country of his own making. To his credit, he jarred it, us, off our axes for a moment, and how many of us can say we've even done that?

But time heals; we've recovered. And like any kind of, not pollution, but, let us say, irregularity, he was in time swept aside by a forgiving natural process. Call it the calming effect of the color green. Though I'm certainly no hard core environmentalist, I CAN appreciate how it covers old tires, how it shades and traverses, takes back even the foulest of streams given centuries enough. Call it the spring factor if you want. Call it baseball. It eclipses our failures, religious illusions, gives us another chance each new year.

Yes, given time it all comes back again, all the hope we've ever known, all the hope we long for. That why I cover the game. It's as universal as it is American. It's what we seek and where we find it. And despite its real world failings, it's as much an answer as you'll ever need.

Title Description of Books by CMJ Associates, inc.

Behold the Man, Simon of Cyrene By Father Martin DePorres

Inspired writing by a gifted new Author. This story shows us the gifts given to Simon. Through carrying the Cross with Jesus, Simon shares with us the gifts we can expect by carrying our daily crosses.

Price $12.25 each

Becoming the Handmaid of the Lord By Dr. Ronda Chervin

The journals of this well known Catholic writer span her family life as wife and mother, mystical graces sustaining her through a mid-life crisis, the suicide of her beloved son, her widowhood and finally a Religious Sister at the age of 58. Insightful, inspiring & challenging. 327 pages of the heart.

Price $13.75 each

Ties that Bind By Ronda Chervin

The story of a Marriage. This beautiful novel presents the wife's point of view and the husbands point of view on the same conflict. The author Dr. Chervin has written many books on Catholic life. Ties that Bind is both funny and inspiring. A great gift for couple thinking about marriage as well.

Price $8.50 each

The Cheese Stands Alone By David Craig

(The formost religious poet of the day) A dynamite account of a radical conversion from the world of drugs to the search for holiness in the Catholic Church. Realism & poetic imagery combine to make this a must for those who want the real thing. Its a rare book that both monastic and charismatic — anyone acquainted with the latter will love the chapter on misguided zeal, aptly titled "Busbey Burkeley."

Price $12.50 each

The History of Eucharistic Adoration By Father John Hardon, S.J.

In an age of widespread confusion and disbelief, this document offers unprecedented clarity in the most important element of our faith. I recommend that it be prayerfully studied and widely circulated. It is thoroughly researched and well documented, and promises to enlight en, instruct and inspire countless souls to an undying love of our Eucharistic Lord.

Price $4.00 each

The Bishop Sheen We Knew By Father Albert Shamon

A booklet filled with little known information from his Vicar, Fr. Albert J.M. Shamon, Bishop Dennis Hickey and Fr. Mike Hogan, the three remaining priests who worked under Bishop Sheen. A chance to see the day to day workings of the acknowledged prophet of our times.

Price $4.00 each

Born, Unborn By Martin Chervin

What if inside this hospital bag, smashed in pieces, crushed to bits, evidence to make one believe God didn't exist. What if, a second time on earth, the Spirit of Mercy was giving birth, end of the voyage down to earth. In this bag, the child Christ returning to us... A second time, crucified.

Price $9.95 each

To order additional copies of this book:

Please complete the form below and send for each copy

CMJ Marian Publishers
P.O. Box 661 • Oak Lawn, IL 60454
call toll free 888-636-6799 or fax 708-636-2855
email jwby@aol.com
www.cmjbooks.com

Name ______________________________

Address ______________________________

City ______________ State _____ Zip _______

Phone ( ) ______________________________

		QUANTITY		SUBTOTAL
Message to the World				
$10.00	x	________	=	$ ________
Children of the Breath				
$14.50	x	________	=	$ ________
Becoming the Handmaid of the Lord				
$13.75	x	________	=	$ ________
Radiating Christ				
$11.00	x	________	=	$ ________
The Cheese Stands Alone				
$12.50	x	________	=	$ ________
The History of Eucharistic Adoration				
$ 4.00	x	________	=	$ ________
The Bishop Sheen We Knew				
$ 4.00	x	________	=	$ ________
Behold the Man!				
$12.25	x	________	=	$ ________
________________				
$__.__	x	________	=	$ ________
+ tax (for Illinois residents only)			=	$ ________
+ 15% for S&H			=	$ ________
TOTAL			=	$ ________

☐ Check # _______ ☐ Visa ☐ MasterCard

Exp. Date __/__/__

Card # ______________________________

____
signature

Many new & exciting releases for Winter 1997

(If you are interested in any or all of these exciting new titles send us your name and address and we can send you a notice of publication with the price.)

By Way of the Cross By Carol J. Ross

Autobiography. When you read By Way of the Cross you will open yourself to tears of empathy and of joy as you see this woman struggling with terribly physical and mental crosses, scooped up into breathtaking visions of the supernatural world. Paperback. Full color photos. 468 pages. $12.50

Lost in the World: Found in Christ By Father Christopher Scadron

The story of a priest ordained at the age of 63 — As a young Jewish man Padre Pio predicated he would become a Priest. After years of floundering and sin as a naval officer and an artist, this unusually gifted and interested man became a priest at 63! A tale all Catholics will find moving and deeply inspiring, it is also a must for any man you know who might be called to the priesthood at an age older than the usual. $12.50

Dancing with God through the Evening of Life
By Mary Anne McCrickard Benas

Unique insight into the world of the hospice worker and the patient relationship. The beautiful faithful outlook of a elderly man dying and the gifts he gives us through this experience. $12.50

The Third Millennium Woman By Patricia Hershwitzky

Consider the sinking feeling many Catholics get when they see literature about preparing for this great event. They expect what they read or pretend to read to be true, but dull as dishwater. By contrast — here is a book that is wildly funny and also profound. Written by a "revert" (born Catholic who left and then returned), it is also ideal as a gift for those many women we know are teetering on the verge of returning Home. $12.50

Messages to the World from the Mother of God

Daily meditative pocketsize prayer book on the monthly messages given the visionaries in Medjugorji for the conversion of the World, back to her son Jesus. These messages for the World started in 1984 till the present. In 1987 the messages began on the 25th of the month (union of two hearts with the 5 wounds of Jesus) thus the 25th. These are from St. James Church in Medjugorji. Great Gift!!! $10.00

Children of the Breath By Martin Chervin

Who would have dared to challenge Creation if, at the close of each new day, God said, "It is perfect." Instead, His lips spoke "It is good. . ." and the serpent was already in Eden. Thus begins Children of the Breath, a startling journey into the desert where Christ was tempted for forty days of darkness and light. With immense clarity, lyricism, and humor, author Martin Chervin has delivered a powerhouse that will engage readers of any faith. $14.50

Radiating Christ By Fr. Raoul Plus, S.J.

To be a "Christ" is the whole meaning of Christianity. To radiate Christ is the whole meaning of the Christian apostolate. But to be a Christ for one's own personal benefit is not enough; we have to Christianize those around us; in a word we have to radiate Christ. $11.00

To order additional copies of this book:

Please complete the form below and send for each copy

CMJ Marian Publishers

P.O. Box 661 • Oak Lawn, IL 60454

call toll free 888-636-6799 or fax 708-636-2855

email jwby@aol.com

www.cmjbooks.com

Name ______________________________

Address ______________________________

City ____________________ State _____ Zip ________

Phone (   ) ______________________________

		QUANTITY		SUBTOTAL
Message to the World				
$10.00	x	________	=	$ ________
Children of the Breath				
$14.50	x	________	=	$ ________
Becoming the Handmaid of the Lord				
$13.75	x	________	=	$ ________
Radiating Christ				
$11.00	x	________	=	$ ________
The Cheese Stands Alone				
$12.50	x	________	=	$ ________
The History of Eucharistic Adoration				
$ 4.00	x	________	=	$ ________
The Bishop Sheen We Knew				
$ 4.00	x	________	=	$ ________
Behold the Man!				
$12.25	x	________	=	$ ________
____________________				
$__.__	x	________	=	$ ________
+ tax (for Illinois residents only)			=	$ ________
+ 15% for S&H			=	$ ________
TOTAL			=	$ ________

☐ Check # ________ ☐ Visa ☐ MasterCard

Exp. Date ___/___/___

Card # ______________________________

____
signature